MEMORIES ARE MADE OF THIS

To celebrate the publication of

Memories

BY
CLAIRE HENNESSY

POOLBEG AND THE BODY SHOP ARE OFFERING YOU
THE CHANCE TO WIN 2 COOL HAMPERS, ONE FOR YOU AND ONE
FOR YOUR BEST FRIEND FOR YOUR NEXT SLEEPOVER

SIMPLY ANSWER THE FOLLOWING QUESTION:
Q. WHO IS THE FOUNDING OWNER OF THE BODY SHOP?

A. _____

ANSWERS ON A POSTCARD CLEARLY MARKED
MEMORIES COMPETITION, TO:
Poolbeg Press, 123 Grange Hill, Baldoyle, Dublin 13

Closing date for all entries 2nd May 2002
The draw will take place on the 8th of May 2002
The first correct entry drawn will win the prize of 2 hampers from The Body Shop.
The judge's decision is final

Memories

Memories

CLAIRE HENNESSY

POOLBEG
FOR CHILDREN

Published 2002
by Poolbeg Press Ltd.
123 Grange Hill, Baldoyle
Dublin 13, Ireland
Email: poolbeg@poolbeg.com
www.poolbeg.com

13 5 7 9 10 8 6 4 2

A catalogue record for this book is available from the British Library.

ISBN 1 84223 098 0

Cover design by DW Design, London
Set by Patricia Hope in Palatino 10.6/15
Printed by Cox & Wyman Ltd.,
Reading, Berkshire

ABOUT THE AUTHOR

Apart from a rather obvious obsession with writing, sixteen-year-old Claire Hennessy loves reading, music (listening to it – people tend to scream and run away when she sings), watching TV, and her friends. She's currently enjoying Transition Year and trying not to think about the dreaded Leaving Cert. She's also the author of *Dear Diary* and *Being Her Sister*. Visit her online at www.clairehennessy.com.

Also by Claire Hennessy
Dear Diary
Being Her Sister

ACKNOWLEDGEMENTS

I'd like to thank everyone who has helped me in the writing of this book – or, at least, helped me not to go crazy while doing so. Thanks to Mom and Dad for letting me stay up late and for providing tea! Thanks to Andrew, Claire, Jenny, Paula and Sam, some really fantastic friends – thanks for the reassurances, especially to Sam for reading as I went along. Thanks to all the relatives on both sides of the family who've always taken an interest. Thanks to everyone in Beaufort, students and staff alike, who have read the books and given me their opinions, it means a lot to me. Thanks to anyone who's ever written or emailed me to tell me you like the books – it keeps me going during the tough times! Finally, thanks to whoever you are, reading this, because it means you've bought the book. You're fantastic!

Part One

Back to School

1

Danielle

God, I hate going back to school after the holidays. It's hell. Torture. You've had freedom all summer and suddenly it's back to the rules and regulations of St Anne's Community School. You're a prisoner, stuck there until the first of June. Trapped there with awful homework and boring classes and nagging teachers with no way out. It's horrible.

My one consolation this year is that it's only Transition Year, and that we don't have important exams coming up. Not that the Junior Cert was important – although from the way the teachers went on you'd swear your life depended on it – but it was kind of stressful. Everyone was going on about how much they hadn't studied, and you just *knew* they'd memorised every little thing on the course and were just trying to be cool. Meanwhile, I *really* hadn't studied. And of course my parents started giving out to me for not working hard. I looked like the bad daughter all of last year, but what else is new? Rachel was always studying. She was incredibly organised about it, too. You know, with a study plan that she actually *followed* (I made out a zillion study plans and spent most of the time colouring them in) and notes from each subject, and copies and sheets dating back to first year.

Sometimes I really don't see how we're related. I mean, if it wasn't for the physical resemblance I'd think one of us – probably me – was adopted. We're both dark-haired with similar features, only she's actually pretty. I spend half my time thinking that maybe I look okay, and the other half searching for a paper bag to put over my head. Rache is the serious student, the girl who freaks out if she gets a B. (If I get a B, I'm ready to throw a party.) She's a mega brain, but I don't hold it against her. Most of the time. She turned fourteen yesterday, on the first of September, but she's going into Transition Year. The scary thing is she could actually be doing fifth year, but she seems to have enough sense not to do something that crazy. Besides, she's changing schools to St Anne's, and we have to do Transition Year. Not that I'm complaining. I would have done it anyway. Third year was hell.

Apart from having wildly different approaches to school, Rache and I get along pretty well. More or less. Sometimes in the sense that less is more. We hang around with the same group most of the time and we're mainly into the same type of music and the same clothes. (Which, incidentally, works out great when I want to borrow a CD or can't find anything to wear.) So that prevents me from killing her when she's really getting on my nerves or when the parents are raving on about how perfect she is. (You know, you'd think they'd have the decency to *pretend* they loved us both equally . . .) Over the years I've accepted the fact that everyone worships the ground my little sister walks on, but sometimes it still gets to me. The annoying thing is, she doesn't seem to realise that she has everything going for her. She'll moan about being too fat or something and I don't know if she really thinks she is or if it's just to get attention and the reassurance that friends and families are practically bound by law to give teenage girls who think they're fat. "Of course not, you look great!"

I used to have to tell that to my friend Nicole constantly, but she got over her "I'm so fat!" stage pretty quickly. Nicole isn't the type to wallow in self-pity for very long. She's got a great outlook on life, or at least she seems to. I don't know – I mean, she's one of my best friends, but there are times when I feel like there's still a lot I don't know about her. She's also very opinionated at times and isn't scared of saying what she thinks, which has led to a couple of fights in the past. She has principles and morals. I don't, not really. I just let things happen.

Like the time I started making up lies about my friend Mark so that Rache would decide to end things with him and then he'd be available so I could go out with him. Probably not my finest moment ever, but I felt bad about it afterwards. Still, I have to admit to getting stupid over guys sometimes. I'll do things that are completely out of character just so they'll like me. A lot of the time when I'm around guys, I'm a completely different person, unless it's a really good friend. Some of my friends are like that, but they're, I don't know, confident enough to not change too much. I suppose the most obvious example is when I started smoking because my boyfriend of the time did too. Most of my friends smoke because they want to, or because everyone's doing it. I started because of a guy. Typical. Then I spent six months trying to quit. Nicole and Rache are vehemently anti-smoking, so that helped. A little. Even though I wanted to kill them when they shook their heads disapprovingly and preached about how bad it was. Yeah, yeah, we all *know* it's a disgusting habit, but it's just so . . . *wonderful*. There are times I still crave them.

Anyway, I think that's all you need to know about me. Danielle Connolly, aged fifteen, a "party animal" according to my parents (which isn't true, I just like to have a good time) and a girl who'll do pretty much anything for a boy she really likes.

Why does that sound so pathetic? I'm a romantic, okay? I believe that having someone in your life is important. Love is everything.

Not that I'm going to find love now that school's started again. Most of the guys in school are okay, but they're either ugly, or idiots. Or else I've gone out with them. I have a history with a lot of the boys I know, most notably Mark. (Tall, dark, and *adorably* cute.) We were together for a year and two months (and five days, two hours and forty minutes, give or take a second or two) in second and third year, and then came to a mutual agreement that we were better off as friends. (Fine, fine. *He* came to the mutual agreement, and I nodded and acted like I'd been thinking

4

the exact same thing to avoid utter humiliation. Such is the world of teen romance.) He was, I guess, the big love of my life for a long time, and even though we're just good friends now, there's still moments (like all the ones where I'm awake, for example) when I miss that. I've been out with a couple of other guys, and met plenty (probably too many) of them, but no one's come close to being as great as he is.

And there I go getting all sappy again. Someone stop me the next time I do that. It's just that it's . . . Mark.

The doorbell's ringing. I'm brushing my hair and graciously let Rachel go and answer it.

"Danielle! Come on!" Rachel yells upstairs.

"Get your ass down here right now!" Nicole adds cheerfully. Way too cheerful for this early in the morning. It's eight-thirty a.m., which is a time I haven't seen on a clock all summer. Nicole's not exactly a morning person either. Usually she doesn't bother calling around before school because she's racing down there five minutes after class has started. It must be a first-day-back thing. Sort of like the way I used to be in primary school – every September I declared that this was the year I was going to have all my homework done and pay attention and not get into trouble. It usually wore off after about two weeks.

I finish brushing out my hair and flip it over my shoulders. I can finally actually flip my hair; it's enough to make me grin even this early in the morning. Every so often I decide I'm fed up with long hair and cut it really short, and then I spend months wishing it'd hurry up and grow back. It's finally past my shoulders and I'm happy with it.

I thunder down the stairs and land beside the two of them, all three of us in our neat and clean school uniforms. We look like innocent schoolgirls who've never been exposed to any impurity in our lives. It's kind of funny. Not that we're all out on the streets selling our bodies or anything, but we're not exactly sheltered from the world. Who our age *is*, these days?

"Off we go, I suppose," Rachel sighs, staring dully at her reflection in the hall mirror.

"Nervous?" Nicole asks.

"No," she shrugs. Lying, however, isn't exactly Rachel's forte. She looks jittery. Then again, this is the first day at a new school for her. In first year, we went to different secondary schools, because our parents thought she'd do better in an all-girls school. I have to say they were probably right, since all the students there do seem to get really good results. Anyway, they didn't really mind what school I went to. Well, they made a half-hearted suggestion that I go to that school, but no one was surprised when I chose to go to the school all my friends were going to. So Rache has spent the last three years there, being a dedicated student, and, if you ask me, not having much fun. I'm not sure why she wanted to change schools, but she convinced Mum and Dad to let her move. Probably because of her friends. Rache is really close to Nicole and Caitlin, who lives down the road, and I get the feeling she was getting bored with her friends at school. Not

6

surprisingly. They're not the most thrilling people ever. They tend to get excited about things like Science homework. As academic as Rache is, I don't think I've ever seen her squeal over working out a chemical equation.

"It'll be fine," Nicole says. "Well, apart from all the guys and the constant sexual innuendo."

"You say that like it's a bad thing," I grin.

Rachel laughs. "I'll cope."

On that note, we set off for school.

2

Nicole

The worst thing about summer is that it has to end. It's never long enough – you want it to last forever. The endless days with no responsibilities, where you can just hang around with your friends without school getting in the way. Of course, a ton of people I knew were working, but that's beside the point. And off on holidays. And I suppose the more you see people, the more they get on your nerves.

Okay, maybe summer wasn't total perfection, but my point is, it's better than school. I spent the last six weeks of third year counting down to June 14, when my last exam would be over and I could escape until September 2nd. And all in all, it was a pretty good summer. I mean, there was heartbreak and emotional trauma, but that's part and parcel of summer, just like the fun and the laughter. For me, anyway – or it was this summer, at least.

I got to have some really good talks with my friends.

(Well, Mark.) You know the way it is when there's a big group of you; a lot of the time you don't really talk about the important things or confide your secrets. And I like having one-on-one conversations every so often. Mark and I had a lot of those. The guy is a lot deeper than I realised. I mean, I thought I knew him pretty well. He's always been one of the guys that I know that I could actually talk to, but there's a lot I didn't know about him. He's more thoughtful than I gave him credit for. Then again, he does act like a typical guy most of the time – for "guy", read "asshole". Danielle is always raving on about how wonderful he is – but Danielle is hopelessly in love with him and not what you'd call unbiased. Most of my friends have fancied Mark at one stage or another; he's just one of those guys that girls like. It's the same with his friend Adam. But they've all gotten over him one way or another. Even I went through the stage, and we went out for a little while – but I don't count it as important, seeing as we were twelve at the time and it was a five-day relationship. Anyway, Danielle's never gotten over him, but then again, I don't think he's ever really got over her, either. He broke up with her, but if you ask me, he regrets it. Although I can't be sure – we never really talk about it. He always changes the subject. And he's back to being a typical guy.

Okay, I'm not going to hide the fact that I think most guys are complete idiots. You might as well know my opinion of half the world's population. Idiots. On the other hand, they're so damned attractive. They draw you to them with their magnetic charm and then are too stupid to realise when you're interested. They flirt with you and then they break your heart.

Not that I'm bitter or anything.

Not at all.

Not one little bit.

Anyway, myself, Rachel and Danielle are on our way to school on the dreaded first day back when we run into a couple of the guys from our year, Mark and Adam among them. I watch as Adam flirts with Rachel and she blushes a little. She's still not that used to attention from guys and sometimes she's unsure how to handle it. After a few moments, though, she's holding her own, and I'm proud of her. In some ways Rache is like a little sister to me – she's inexperienced in a lot of things. In other ways she's just one of my best friends. She's younger than I am, but she's not stupid. She knows what she's talking about. Still, there are some things that I don't talk to her about. I don't go to her with every problem that I have, but I do listen to hers. I guess there are just some things that I don't want to tell my friends about. Like Niall. That was something that no one knows about. Well, except Mark, and I'm still not sure whether I should have told him or not. I mean, I needed to talk to *someone* – but at the same time, I'm a little ashamed, or embarrassed, about what happened, about what a fool I made of myself.

You know, we really don't need to be discussing this now . . .

Back to Rachel and Adam, and away from me. I don't mind having the focus on me as long as it's on the outside me, the mask that I wear the entire time and not the real Nicole that dwells within. The confident Nicole who's always up for some fun and always ready to cause trouble if it's an issue she feels strongly about – that's the girl that people know and, most of the time, like. She pretends to have more confidence than she really does, and she acts more sure of what she believes than she is, in the hope that she can convince other people.

Rachel! Adam! Pay attention, Nic. We walk into the classroom and Rache dumps her bag down on a chair. He looks like he wants to sit next to her, but settles for behind, just so he doesn't look too eager, I suppose. I sit beside her, and Danielle, tossing her hair, sits in front. Because she knows the closer she is to the front, the more guys will be looking at her. At least that's what I think. I can see some new boy at the other side of the classroom ogling her already. Yep, school has begun.

Guys like Danielle. Not only is she pretty, but she oozes confidence. They're drawn to her like moths to a flame or chocoholics to Cadbury's. She likes it when they have crushes on her, and I think that's part of her attraction. There's this feel-good factor involved – they flirt, she smiles, and they're on top of the world. She's *nice* to them. Most of the time I'm not. At least that's my way of explaining why she has more admirers than I do. It's easier than thinking it's because she's prettier or skinnier or whatever. I've been in the stage where you think life would be so much better if you were skinny, and it just makes you miserable, always worrying about whether you look fat or how many calories are in this, that or the other. I'm glad I'm past that phase. If a guy prefers your skinnier friend over you simply because she's thin, he's not worth it.

In my opinion, most of the males on the planet aren't worth it anyway, but that's beside the point.

A teacher comes in. She looks new. Young, scared. I give her three weeks before she has a nervous breakdown. "Y-y-you've to go d-d-down to the hall for an as-assembly," she stammers.

No one listens to her. They're either too busy talking to their friends or deliberately ignoring her. Oh God, she looks like she wants to run away. And I want to hug her.

Two fingers in my mouth, and I whistle. "Guys, shut up!" I yell. And there's silence, or what passes for it at this school.

"Down to the assembly hall," Little Miss Nerves repeats, a little more confident this time.

As we all leave the classroom, Mark murmurs, "Nicole, patron saint of new teachers."

"Oh, shut up," I snap.

"You've gotta do something about that attitude, Nic. No wonder you don't have a boyfriend."

I stare at him in disbelief. "That was low."

He has the grace to look ashamed. "Yeah, I know. Sorry."

I'm still hurt by him throwing the fact that I don't have a boyfriend in my face. After me telling him about Niall, all those long conversations . . . and he says something stupid like that.

"Hey." He puts his hand on my arm. "Ignore what I said, okay? I'm just a guy . . . one of those idiots, remember?"

I smile. "How could I forget?"

"You coming?" Danielle calls from halfway down the corridor.

"Suppose we have to," I sigh, and Mark and I follow the gang down to the hall.

3

Rachel

"Well, that's forty-seven minutes of my life wasted that I want back," Nicole rolls her eyes after assembly. We got a talk on TY – why we should try to make the most of it, and not think of it as a doss year, but throw ourselves into it and get as much out of it as possible.

Naturally we all came out of it thinking, this is going to be a doss year.

We're teenagers. Lazy. What do they expect?

I used to care about things like school, and try and work hard. But lately it's all become so boring. Like, last year. I'd go up to my room to study and end up doodling on the books for two hours. I tried to study as much as I could – but I just got so fed up of it all. And my parents were expecting me to do so well.

Danielle, my sister, doesn't know how easy she has it. They don't care how she does. Well, they care, but they don't expect as much from her as they do from me. I have to do brilliantly. She has to pass, and they're happy.

I hate it.

"That was so boring!" Naomi agrees. Naomi, who missed half of it because she got into school late. She didn't even get given out to – just looked sweet and innocent and sat down beside the rest of us. I'm not surprised, with those big blue eyes and blonde hair. She looks like an angel. She acts like a devil. It's an interesting combination.

She's pretty, though. Most of my sister's friends are. Danielle is, too. It's sort of depressing to be constantly surrounded by people more attractive than you are. You're the ugly duckling amid swans.

Oh, who am I kidding? It's *incredibly* depressing. I mean, when I look in the mirror, I want to turn away in disgust, but there's some little part of me that likes tormenting myself and forces me to stay and stare in dismay at my reflection, like the way you have to look at an accident on the road. Morbid curiosity. The longer I look, the worse it gets and the more faults I see. The monster stares back at me, growing more hideous by the second, until finally I have to drag myself away.

I know most people aren't happy with the way they look, but I seriously can't imagine Danielle avoiding mirrors half the time just so she doesn't have to catch a glimpse of her reflection, or Nicole staring into one and finding a zillion things wrong with her appearance.

But then, they don't have anything to worry about when it comes to the way they look. Beautiful. Skinny. They can eat whatever they want without having to worry about getting fat. They don't even think about it. Naomi is a total chocoholic and she's still tiny. Danielle eats tons, but she never seems to gain any weight. And Caitlin is even worse. She doesn't seem to get hungry at all – she just eats when she's reminded to. I would love to be like that, but I get hungry – and usually head straight for the chocolate or the crisps. Caitlin's one of those people who realises at dinner time that she hasn't eaten all day and probably should. I'm envious.

I get jealous a lot, I guess. I think everyone else has a better life than I do, but it's because it's true – they do. They always seem so happy and carefree. I'm not like that. I try to be, but sometimes it's just so hard and I don't see the point in bothering, because trying to fit in is a pointless exercise anyway – I never will. I never fit in anywhere. I mean, I didn't fit in when I was in primary school, not really. I didn't fit in with my friends in my old school. And I don't really fit in with Danielle and her friends. They're nice most of the time, but they don't really want me around. Most people don't.

I do have a plan, you know. I don't want to be the outsider my entire life. No one does. It's pretty simple. I just need to be thin. You think I'm stupid, okay. Hear me out. A lot of the way I feel about myself has to do with the way I look. And if I was thinner – well, I'd be happier, right? I'd feel more confident, and I'd make friends more easily, and people would like the thin Rachel better than the old chubbier one, because she'd be cooler and prettier.

And that's all I have to do – lose weight, and everything else in my life falls into place. Unfortunately losing weight is a lot harder than it sounds. I mean, I like food. And I *love* junk food. And it's harder to stay away from it than I thought it would be.

Maybe I'll just fail at this, like I do with everything else. Rachel Connolly can do well in school, but when it comes to every other aspect of living, she fails miserably. She's a pathetic loser. No wonder no one likes her.

You know, I swore I wasn't going to be one of those teenagers who have no self-esteem and feel that the world's against them. I *promised* myself I wasn't going to be the stereotype.

And I've been a teenager for barely a year and already I'm depressed and angst-ridden.

The difference is my life really is bad. I mean, not bad in a lot of ways. Like, I have a stable home environment. It's not like I have parents walking out or a situation with domestic violence or anything. And it's not like I cut myself or anything. I'm not suicidal. But it's not exactly wonderful, is it?

I feel like crap. Worthless. Unwanted. Sometimes I'm happy – but those times are becoming more and more infrequent.

And you know, no one notices. I mean, *no one notices!* No one seems to realise how bad I feel, or maybe it's just that they don't care. Danielle hasn't asked me am I okay, and Nicole, who I've always thought is one of the most sensitive people I know, and who is *meant* to be one of my best friends, hasn't checked to see if something's wrong.

I guess their lives are so perfect they don't want to deal with little inconveniences like me. I don't count as a real person, right?

4

Danielle

Actually there's another consolation on this, our first day
back, and it's that we finish at twelve. I've been counting
down to noon since nine-thirty. It feels like we've already
been in school forever instead of a couple of hours, even
though we haven't really done any work. We got a pep talk
on how we should take advantage of this year to get
involved and *participate* in activities, seeing as how the
academic work is going to be minimal. It was sickening. Ms
Vaughan trying to be cool and one of us as she yapped on,
and failing miserably. Then we went to whatever module
we'd picked and got a talk on what we'd be doing until the
midterm break. I'm doing Art. It's going to be such a doss.
Nicole took it for Junior Cert and was one of the very few
people who didn't hate all the pressure and work, so she's
in the class too, mainly because she thought the other
options were crap. Rache picked it, too, which is cool. I
mean, she's my sister and we fight a lot, but I'm glad she's

there. I can keep an eye on her; make sure she's doing okay. Most of the people in our year are all right, but there are some people that, well, aren't. And Rachel doesn't always stand up for herself when she should. I can't really blame her, I don't always either – but she's more sensitive. Nicole, on the other hand, doesn't take crap from anyone, which I guess is why some people are intimidated by her. And Naomi doesn't have to stand up for herself, because she looks so utterly angelic that no one would ever be mean to her. Although she would, if she had to. She's nowhere near as sweet as she looks and inside she's capable of being one of the bitchiest people I know. Which is why I'm glad I'm her friend and not her enemy.

Most of us hang out on the green down the road from the school once we're set free, although a few of my friends – Tara, Jenny, Grace, Liz – are going shopping. It's weird the way friendships change over the years. Grace and Caitlin used to be so close, but then Grace met Robbie while Caitlin was still with him, and now they barely talk. And Jenny and Naomi were once like Siamese twins, but once Jenny got more confidence, she stopped hanging out with Naomi the whole time, who, admittedly, did take advantage of Jenny's shyness. We all used to be a lot closer, but now I barely talk to them outside of school. I don't even know what they did all summer. I was hanging out with Naomi, Caitlin, Michelle and Rache most of the time. Michelle doesn't go to our school, but she lives nearby, and Rachel knows her really well. She's the sister of this guy, Eric, in our class, so we sort-of knew her. Anyway, she spent a lot of time with us this summer. It was fun. We had water fights and acted like kids, and we'd lie out on the grass and talk about boys and life, and although we weren't really *doing* anything, we all had a great time. We never do that during school time – it's the sort of thing you only do in summer.

It was only in the last couple of weeks that we didn't see each other so often. Michelle went to Cork for a few days, and Caitlin was babysitting, and Naomi was – actually, I have no idea where Naomi was. She can be very secretive sometimes. Anyway, I just lounged around the house, watching TV and stuffing my face. Rachel did the same, except she wasn't stuffing her face – she was counting calories. She was doing the "I'm too fat!" thing and even though I told her she wasn't, she started dieting anyway. She doesn't seem to have kept it up, though. Mum groaned when she heard Rachel was on a diet – she doesn't get how Rache can be so smart and still think she needs to diet. Actually, I don't get it either. If I had Rachel's brains, I'd be happy. I mean, she doesn't need to work so hard to get good grades – she works hard just to make sure. I'd love to be that intelligent, but I guess we can't have everything, right?

Anyway, there's a bunch of us lying and sitting on the grass, and it could almost be summer again, except for a lot more people and the addition of school bags and uniforms.

"Art seems like it's going to be a doss," I say to Nicole, who's sitting next to me.

She nods. "I know. I feel sorry for Miss Morgan, though."

Miss Morgan's new this year and you can tell it's

probably her first year teaching. She came into the class this morning to tell us to go down to the hall, and she had "Pick on me!" written all over her. She's nice, but desperately lacking in confidence. I bet she'll let the class walk all over her. We tend to do that a lot.

"Mmm. She'll want to quit by Christmas."

"She's so nice, though," Nicole sighs. "It's a pity. Oh, well. Not like we can do anything about it."

I laugh. "Nic, if anyone's too mean to her, you're going to do something about it and you know it. You're that type."

She grins. "Ah, you know me so well. So, what have you been up to all summer? I barely saw you."

"Just hanging around."

"Me too. I was talking to Mark a lot."

"Mark?" I ask. I'm slightly jealous. I didn't get to spend much time with Mark at all.

"Yeah," she smiles. "Just talking, Danielle. I don't fancy him."

I sigh. "Is it that obvious?"

"Obvious you're head-over-heels, madly-truly-deeply in love with him? What makes you say that?" she smirks.

"As long as he doesn't know," I say. If Mark found out I still like him . . . well, it'd be weird. Unless he likes me. That'd be different.

"He's a guy. Do you *think* he sees what's right in front of him?"

"Don't tell me you're turning into a vicious man-hater, Nic."

"Nah, just stating a fact. Hey, do you think Adam likes Rache?"

"Maybe." I look over at where he's sitting, talking to Naomi, smiling. "Or maybe he likes Naomi."

She follows my gaze. "Naomi doesn't look too interested. Surprise, surprise."

"Why surprise, surprise?"

"Well, when was the last time you saw Naomi interested in *any* guy, Danielle?" she asks.

I shrug. "I don't know . . . Nic!" And her not-so-subtle message finally gets through to my brain. "Come on, it's Naomi we're talking about. I don't think . . ." I never even thought about it like that. Naomi is just independent. She likes her space. She's too mature for the boys we know. I know her too well for her to be keeping a secret that big from me.

Nicole is silent. "I don't know. I've tried asking her, but she tends to avoid the subject. Besides, it's none of my business. She's my friend, but if she doesn't want to talk about it, I'm not going to force her."

I say the first thing that comes into my head. "Nic, you sound like such a *grown-up*."

She giggles. "Yeah, that's me."

"Heya," Mark comes over and sits next to us. "Thought I'd spend some time with my two favourite girls."

"We're honoured by your presence," Nicole laughs.

"We're not worthy," I add.

He grins. "Yeah, I know you love me. So what's up?"

"Airplanes. Birds. Umbrellas." This is from Nicole, deliberately taking his question literally to piss him off.

He mock-glares at her. She pulls a Naomi and gazes at him oh-so-innocently.

They're practically flirting. It's disgusting. Oh God, what if he likes her? I mean, what if he really, really likes her? What if he loves her? What if he plans to marry her and have six kids and have a house and a dog and a car and . . .

Breathe. They're not going to get married.

Not if I have anything to say about it, anyway.

5

Nicole

"She looks pissed off with one or more of us," I say to Mark. Danielle is over on the other side of the green, talking to Caitlin, but she glances over every so often. I get the feeling she only went over there in the hope that either me or Mark would beg "No, Danielle, please stay here. We're so fortunate to have you speak to us lowly beings" and she's annoyed that we didn't, but just went on talking.

He sighs. "I know. You think I should talk to her?"

He is *way* too nice for his own good.

"She'll get over it. She's just in a bit of a huff. She thinks I fancy you, I think."

"Do you?" he grins.

"Of course not. You're too nice. I only fancy assholes, remember? The ones who inevitably break my heart?"

He doesn't say anything, and I'm sorry for mentioning it. Why do I do this? If I just keep my problems to myself then everything's fine and no one knows what's really going on in my mind. Mark knows too much about me, that's the problem. It makes me vulnerable.

"Did you tell Rache or Danielle about Niall?" he finally asks.

I shake my head. "No. It's not that important. There's not much point."

"Not that important?" he repeats sceptically. *"Right."*

"It isn't . . . oh, look, it's not something that I want to tell them, okay?" I finally snap.

"But they're like, your best friends." He sounds puzzled.

"Yeah, I know, but . . . I still don't want them to know. I made a fool of myself and I paid the price. It'd be worse if they knew. I mean, Danielle would probably just laugh at me for being such an idiot."

"No, she wouldn't," he says automatically. Then he considers it. "Well, Rachel wouldn't."

"No, Rachel would be disgusted with me, and that'd be even worse."

"Nic – what happened with Niall still bothers you."

"What are you talking about?" I demand. "It doesn't! No way."

"Oh, yeah, sure. Remember this morning? You completely freaked out."

"That was different. That was about me and my general lack of success with guys."

"General meaning Niall."

"No!" I snap, but I know he's right. I just want to argue

this case so that he won't start getting at me for not telling Rachel or Danielle or Naomi or anyone. I don't want to tell them. I can't.

He shrugs. "Okay. Whatever you say."

"Stop patronising me."

"Was I?" he asks innocently.

I glare at him. "Mark. You are the one person in the world who knows about what happened between me and Niall and considering the way you're acting right now, I'm thinking that's one person too many."

He starts to protest, but I'm already getting my schoolbag and saying bye to everyone else. Rachel offers to walk home with me.

"So, what was going on with you and Mark?" she asks, flipping her hair over her shoulder. It's a natural gesture as opposed to the flirty way Danielle does it, and it makes me wonder how the guys can prefer Danielle to Rache. Rache is like the inside-me; Danielle is more like outer-me. I guess that's partly why I like Rachel better.

"Just talking," I reply.

"You looked like you were fighting."

"Yeah, that too."

"Don't tell me. He's having an affair and leaving you to raise the kids all by yourself."

"That's exactly it. No, it was just over some stupid stuff that happened this summer. Nothing important."

"You spent a lot of time with him over the summer, huh?" she asks.

I nod. "Yeah. I probably should have spent more time

with you and Naomi and everyone, but . . . I don't know. Mark and I did a lot of talking. Once we started we could go on forever."

She smiles. "That's pretty much what we did most of the time, too. Me, Danielle, Naomi, Caitlin and Michelle."

"Michelle? Eric's sister?"

Rachel nods. "Yeah. You know her, right?"

"Yeah." She used to be Rachel's best friend in primary school. I'm kind of annoyed that she was the one hanging out with them this summer instead of me. It's easier to be annoyed at her than at myself. I was just down the road most of the time, I could have been talking to them. But no, I was spilling my guts to Mark. When I wasn't throwing myself at Niall, obviously.

There we go again. Niall comes up once more. I'm trying to forget about him but he always manages to worm his way into my thoughts. Typical.

We walk in silence for a couple of minutes.

"You want to come over to my house?" I invite.

She shakes her head. "No, I think I'll just go home."

"Okay," I nod. She obviously wants to be on her own. No problem. I'm not going to pressurise her.

As we say goodbye and I head towards my house, I start thinking about Niall, as usual. At first it's just a few "Mmmm . . . he's so gorgeous" thoughts. He is, really. Eighteen. Tall. Fair. Not skinny but not all muscle either – sort of *lean*. And absolutely divine.

He's a friend of a friend, that friend being this guy I knew in primary school and ran into over the summer. We were introduced, and I knew this was it. Niall was someone really special.

Don't laugh. I never thought I could be so head-over-heels in love with someone. The boyfriends I'd had have been nice, but that was it. I liked them while I was with them, but once it was over, I got over it pretty quickly. I never understood how some of my friends, like Danielle, would do anything to impress someone they fancied.

But with Niall – I started to get it. I'd do anything to get him to like me.

I flirted and flirted, and to tell you the truth, he seemed pretty interested. I got pretty confident. I was sure he liked me and that it was just a matter of time before he confessed his feelings for me. The fact that he was holding back was just part of his natural reserve. He was scared in case I'd reject him. Maybe he'd even had a bad experience with a girl before – someone who had broken his heart, and he still hadn't fully recovered. But I would help him to heal.

Total crap.

I was in town one day with my half-sister, Valerie, when I saw him kissing another girl. I think that was the worst moment of my life, seeing them together. That night, every time I closed my eyes, I saw the two of them, like it was an image imprinted on my inner eyelids. But right then, I didn't say anything, even though I could feel tears welling up in my eyes. Valerie continued babbling on in her chirpy way about the top she'd just bought, and how great it was that she'd waited until the sale to buy it, seeing as she'd got it for half-price, and by the time she actually looked at me, we were halfway down the street and I was a little calmer, at least on the surface.

Inside, I was still in complete and utter turmoil. But I'm used to wearing a mask, and this one was one of utter tranquillity and nonchalance.

Sometimes I think that it would have been a good thing if I was in the habit of telling my friends everything. Then maybe what happened next could have been avoided, and I wouldn't be still thinking about Niall weeks later, replaying incidents in my head.

6

Rachel

Nicole didn't even *question* me when I said I just wanted to go home. I mean, she just *accepted* it. She didn't ask, "Are you sure?" or say, "Okay, I'll call you later then" or anything. Just said, "Okay" and then, "Bye, see ya tomorrow."

I'm pretty sure she didn't even want to walk home with me. It's not like she invited me or anything. I just said I'd walk with her, and it was really so that I could get home before Mum does. She works nine-to-two as a receptionist, and I didn't want her there when I got in.

I open the door, pick up the post, and leave it on the table in the hall. Into the kitchen, get a glass of water. I'm absolutely starving. I ate nothing at break – Mum gave me a lunch but it's in the bin. I was hoping I could get through the day without eating anything. I had this plan where I'd leave crumbs on a plate in the sink and tell Mum I had lunch before she got home, and then I could get away without eating until dinner. But I didn't count on being so

31

hungry. Or what happened with Nicole. Or feeling like crap because I don't feel like I'm ever going to fit in at school. Or thinking that I'm completely worthless.

I know I shouldn't eat anything if I want to be thin. But right now, I want to. I *need* to. There's biscuits in the kitchen that I'm not going to touch, because me and Danielle are the only ones who eat them, and she'll know that I've been stuffing myself and that I'm a greedy pig.

I have to keep my lack of self-control a secret. That's why there's chocolate in my room, hidden away at the back of my wardrobe. I know it shouldn't be there. I bought it and I know I should have thrown it out. But I just couldn't bear to. So it's there, and right now, I'm glad of it.

Two bars in, and I'm feeling better. This is good; everything's going to be okay. Four bars in and a twinge of guilt seeps in, but I push it away. Six bars in and I'm feeling a little sick, a combination of the chocolate overdose and the guilt.

I stare at the empty wrappers in horror. God. I'm disgusting. I have to get rid of the evidence. I crumple them up and throw them in the bin, but that doesn't make the guilt go away. How am I supposed to get thin if I keep doing this?

I know what I have to do, of course. It's not the first time I've done it. And maybe this is also why I wanted to be home before Mum – so I could do this in peace without worrying about her hearing.

Even so, I automatically turn on the taps before I kneel on the cold tiled floor of the bathroom. Fingers down my throat, fighting all my natural reflexes as I push them down far enough. Then I throw up into the toilet, gagging until I'm sure my stomach's empty and all the chocolate is gone.

There we go. All better now.

"Hey," Danielle greets me, coming home half an hour later.

"Heya," I reply.

"Mum home?"

"Yeah, she's upstairs."

Danielle flops down on the couch beside me. "Did you *see* Mark and Nicole?" she demands.

I was hoping to hear something along the lines of "Hey, sis, I'm worried about you. Is everything okay?" or "Hey Rache, we need to talk. I'm scared you're doing something stupid, you know?" or "Rachel, I just want you to know that I'm here for you".

"Yeah," I say, giving up all hope of Danielle being a concerned and selfless big sister.

"Flirt, flirt, flirt," she mutters. "I mean, what's she doing hanging around with him? They haven't had a civil conversation in months. Years. What happened?"

"They spent time together over the summer," I remind her. "They're getting along now."

"Getting along? That's a nice way of putting it," she scowls.

"Danielle . . ." I sigh. "Mark isn't your personal property. He's not even your boyfriend. He's allowed to talk to other girls."

Just like me, Naomi, Caitlin and Michelle told her

repeatedly over the summer while she babbled on about how wonderful he is, but she never seems to listen to us. *Any* of us, but especially me. I'm just her stupid little sister who doesn't know anything about boys and relationships.

"Maybe I should get a collar and a leash for him," she muses. "You know, that way I could keep him away from other girls." She's in joke mood now, the worst of it is over.

"I'm sure he'd love that idea," I reply sarcastically.

Silence. She's bored already. Five minutes with Rachel and the conversation ends. I leave first.

"Where're you going?" she asks.

"My room," I reply. Where I can get away from the world. Listen to music, close my eyes, daydream. Only when I open my eyes or the CD ends, I'm back where I started. Fat, ugly, dull Rachel Connolly.

I have to keep on focussing on the solution. The word echoes in my mind, the magical four-letter word.

Thin. Thin. Thin.

7

Danielle

Once Rachel's gone up to her room, I don't know what to do. I turn on the TV and flip through the channels. Nothing's on. Nothing I'd watch, anyway. I turn it off again.

I'm a little annoyed. I did want to talk to Rachel about Mark and Nicole. Except she doesn't take my feelings for him seriously. None of them do. Even if she doesn't, I wanted to be told that the flirting didn't mean anything, that it was just something between friends. I wanted to hear that Nicole told Rachel while they were walking home that there was no way she was interested in Mark. Something to that effect.

Sigh. I guess that won't be happening. Oh well, I'll live.

I'm about to get on the phone to call Mark and flirt, or call Adam and see if he knows who Mark is interested in, or call someone, anyone to relieve my boredom, when Mum ropes me into helping her with dinner. Fantabulous.

Meanwhile Princess Rachel is in her room listening to music. (She's gotten into Sarah McLachlan lately, which she calls inspiring and which I call music to slash your wrists by.) I ask Mum why Rachel can't help with the dinner.

"Why would I need Rachel's help? Two of us is fine," she replies. Missing the point entirely and probably deliberately. Just another example of a society (well, family) that places academic excellence ahead of more important talents. Like social skills. And kissing. Mum will thank me when I give her grandchildren to dote over in her old age and Rachel still has her nose stuck in a book.

Michelle calls around after dinner. Rachel has gone to the supermarket with Dad, presumably to make sure he buys low-fat this and diet that. I assume it's Rache she wants, but she grins. "You're not going to get rid of me that easily."

I laugh. "I guess I'll have to put up with you."

When we're up in my room, away from Mum watching the oh-so-fascinating news downstairs, I ask her how her first day back at school was.

"Not exactly fun," she sighs. "Remind me again why I go to a school that doesn't do Transition Year?"

"Because a long, long time ago when we were all deciding what secondary schools to go to, your parents said that a Gaelscoil would be a great idea, and you, being the good child, nodded and said you'd give it a try."

"Of course. I hate being the good one," she grins. "I'm going to kill Eric. Still, he's pissed off with me because I'm going to finish school before he does, and I'm the baby."

Eric is older than Michelle but not by much. He was sixteen last June; she turned fifteen in May. They were really close as kids so their mum sent them off to school at the same time. Michelle was in Rachel's class in primary school. Eric was in mine – we used to compare "annoying little sister" stories. Strangely enough, even after hearing about what a brat Rachel was, he went out with her when she was twelve for six months. They're still friends, as far as I know, anyway.

I laugh. "When's he back from Spain, anyway?"

"He comes back tomorrow. He's probably not going to bother going into school until Thursday. It's so unfair. *He* gets to go off to a foreign country with a couple of his friends, and *I* get sent down to Cork to baby-sit my cousin Allie, the child from hell."

"That's what happens when you're the good child," I smile.

"I'll have to work on that. Maybe if I murdered Eric? Then I'd be an *only* child," she muses. "So, how was your day at school, anyway?"

"It was okay. They keep telling us that we should take fourth year seriously. I don't think it's going to happen."

"Nah, I don't see it happening either."

"I think Mark likes Nicole."

"Seriously? She wouldn't do anything about it, though, would she? I mean, she has to know that you still like him."

I grin at that. "She does, yeah." I've realised that most of the world is aware of this fact, with the exception of Mark. I'm glad that he doesn't realise when I think he doesn't like

37

me back, but if I think he does then I curse his obliviousness.

"I don't really know Nicole, but she's one of your best friends, right? She's not going to want to go after Mark even if she does fancy him, not if she knows you'd be upset about it."

"Unless she thinks that it's time for me to get over Mark and that I should move on," I say, and as soon as the words are out of my mouth I realise that Nicole probably does think that.

"Do you think she does?" Michelle asks.

I shrug. "Maybe. She's the sort of person who doesn't get emotional over guys. If she's going out with someone, fine; if she's not then she won't complain about it or pine for someone. You know what I mean?"

"Yeah. But you and Mark – come on, that's special. It's like Mulder and Scully. Rachel and Ross. Dawson and Joey." I grin at the comparisons as she continues. "Everyone knows you two will probably get back together at some stage. It's not something you can get over."

I stare at her in surprise. "You've changed. You spent most of the summer agreeing with the others that I had to get over him."

"I didn't say get over, I said not to act like you own him. There's a difference. Let him go. He'll come back." She seems pretty confident of this fact.

"You should be an agony aunt," I smile. "How come everyone I know seems to be so good at giving out advice? I'm hopeless at deciding what I should do, never mind what someone else should."

"It's easy to sort out other people's lives," she responds. "Your own life is a lot harder."

"So I've noticed."

"He will come back to you, you know."

"Nicole's really pretty."

"So are you."

"She's got loads of confidence."

"So do you."

"She's blonde."

"Blondes are bimbos."

"You're blonde."

"You're proving my point."

I laugh. She's not a bimbo, and she knows it. But she is trying to make me feel better. It's working. A little bit. Maybe Mark isn't a lost cause after all.

8

Nicole

When I get home, I discover that Valerie is staying with us until she goes back to college, at which point she's moving in with her boyfriend.

She's had yet another fight with her mother. It's like running away in a sense, if it counts as running away when you're nineteen.

Val is the daughter my dad had before he married my mother, the daughter he didn't find out about until she was six years old. Her mum is a bit of a headcase, she told me once, in the same cheerful tone she always uses. She gets on really well with all of my family – better than I do, in fact. Dad adores her, naturally. Mum thinks she's a "lovely girl". Luke, who's nine, worships her because she acts interested in whatever his latest obsession is – Pokemon, Eminem, skateboarding. And I go shopping with her. She's so enthusiastic the whole time. It's exhausting.

"Hey, Nicole!" She bounces down the stairs and envelops me in a hug.

"Val. What are you doing here?" I ask, returning the hug but still a little surprised to see her. Usually if she's staying with us we know about it well in advance. Unless it's a fight.

"The usual. Mam started a fight, and I got out of there."

"What happened?"

"She found a pregnancy test, assumed the worst, called me a slut for having premarital sex and told me I'd be better off as a prostitute than getting a degree."

"Was it yours?"

"The test? Oh yeah. False alarm, though. Thank God. Can you picture me with a baby?" She laughs. "Anyway, don't mention that to your mam or dad. They don't know what the fight was about, and they'd be shocked."

"I'm pretty sure they realise that you and Paul haven't spent the last year holding hands, Val."

"You'd be surprised. They like to think I'm a good little girl. Come on, they still think you've never had a boyfriend. Parents want to believe that their kids are innocent. It's easier for them."

I wonder what they'd think if they knew what had happened with Niall.

After I saw him with that other girl I couldn't get it out of my head. The world had shrunk to encompass that situation only. I wondered who she was, how old she was, whether they had a relationship or not, how old he'd known her, whether he really liked her or not . . .

I had spent so much time working on getting him to like me. I thought he did. The more I thought about it, the more

I realised that he had to. I convinced myself he didn't really like this other girl, she was just convenient. She'd thrown herself at him and he hadn't known how else to respond without hurting her feelings. It was really me that he loved, and he regretted having ever kissed her.

I showed up at his house. He was surprised to see me. Of course he was. He'd never actually given me his address and had only vaguely referred to where he lived. I'd looked it up in the phone book.

And then came Nicole Robinson's pathetic attempt to seduce an older guy. I threw myself at him like I had imagined the other girl had. Compliments and flirtatious remarks spilling out of my mouth. Then, as he didn't seem interested, I begged him. "I thought you liked me, Niall." I sounded so pathetic that I hate to think of it even now. I said I'd do anything for him. Anything.

And you know, he let me go ahead. I had half his clothes off before he realised I was serious, and pushed me away in disgust.

"God, Nicole, get a grip!" he said, straightening his clothes. "What the hell is *wrong* with you?"

I didn't know what to say. I'd never been so *humiliated*. I'd never been rejected like that. I had never, ever offered to sleep with someone just to get them to like me.

I didn't even know him that well. I knew he was gorgeous and that he laughed at my jokes and sometimes went along with my flirting. But I'd never had a serious conversation with him, never really knew how his mind worked and how he felt about things. And I was still so crazy about him that I lowered myself to trying to get him into bed with me in the chance that I could convince him we were really right for each other, even though I knew he was with someone else. He was eighteen, for God's sake. He was finished school already and out in the world while I had only finished my Junior Cert. I was just a stupid kid.

The way he looked at me haunts me. That expression of utter disgust. Although I can't really blame him. I was disgusted at *myself*. But mostly I was hurt that he didn't want me.

I wanted him to be crazy about me the way I was about him.

I went home and cried for hours.

Rejection shakes you up. It makes you question everything about yourself and wonder why you weren't good enough. Was it the way you looked? Was your hair wrong? Were you just plain ugly? Too fat? Too thin? Were you boring, or clingy, or needy? Were you weird?

"Nic, maybe it wasn't anything about you. Maybe it was *him*," Mark told me one day in August, nearly a month after it happened.

I wanted to believe that then and I want to believe it now. I want to believe that I'm a good person and that he was the idiot for not seeing that. I want to believe that guys aren't worth it. But when it comes to Niall, everything I've ever thought doesn't seem to apply to him.

I hate him for that.

I'm still crazy about him, though.

9

Rachel

"Anyone know when Eric's coming back?" Naomi asks at lunchtime. We're sitting outside munching on crisps and popcorn and chocolate, as well as the occasional healthy sandwich, taking advantage of the few sunny days left. I'm not eating anything, of course.

"He comes back today, but Michelle said he'll probably take Wednesday off," Danielle says through a mouthful of popcorn.

"Were you talking to Michelle?" Caitlin asks. Exactly what I'm wondering.

"Yeah, she came around last night," Danielle responds. Still eating her popcorn.

"I haven't seen her since she went to Cork," Caitlin muses.

She came around last night? I didn't know about this. I guess it could have been while I was doing the shopping with Dad, but you'd think she'd wait to say hi to me. She was my best friend for years, after all. Danielle doesn't even know her that well.

"Want a crisp?" Nicole offers.

I shake my head.

"Go on. It won't hurt you," she encourages.

I take one. I'm starving and jealous, a bad combination. One crisp isn't enough and I suddenly want more. Lots more. I'm such a pig, I think. Such a greedy pig. No wonder Michelle prefers to hang out with my sister.

Still, I'm really hungry. "I'm going to the shop. Anyone want to come?" I ask, not really expecting an answer.

Adam leaps up. "Yeah, sure."

I can see Nicole grinning. I know what she's thinking, but it's ridiculous to assume that just because Adam is occasionally friendly towards me that he likes me. He just feels sorry for me. There's no way he could actually be interested. Besides, he probably just wanted to go to the shop anyway and was waiting for someone else.

As we walk off, he turns to me. "Great weather, isn't it?"

I groan. "I'm so boring we have to discuss the *weather*?" As soon as the words are out of my mouth, I want to take them back. I'm so used to worrying about the right thing to say that I hardly ever speak without thinking, or rather, say whatever pops into my mouth.

He laughs. (What a relief. I was scared he'd think I was a total psycho. Maybe he's just being nice to the poor fat girl.)

"Okay, okay," he says. "I was just trying to start a conversation. We did the music one yesterday, remember? Let's see . . . how is Rachel settling in at school so far?"

"It's fine," I shrug. "It's a *school*, you know . . . they're all the same. Boring."

"Yeah, I know what you mean," he says, acting like I've said something really deep and meaningful. If I didn't know better I'd start thinking Nicole was right.

Of course she's wrong, I realise as I'm puking my guts up twenty minutes later. She has to be. There's no point getting my hopes up, because you just end up disappointed and miserable.

10

Danielle

Double English, Wednesday morning. I spend the class drawing on my homework journal. Rachel spends it being attentive. Caitlin spends it texting Naomi and Sean. (Yeah, the point of that eludes me, too.) Nicole spends it whispering to Mark at the back of the classroom. I am seething.

Computers. I spend the class not having any idea what we're meant to be doing and watching the Nicole-and-Mark show.

"Rache, what are we meant to be doing?" I finally ask.

She shrugs. I practically have a heart attack. "You're meant to know these things. You *always* know."

"I don't, okay?" she snaps.

"Fine," I say sulkily, and then get yelled at by the teacher for talking. Fantastic.

Breaktime. I drag Mark away from Adam and Robbie.

"Hey, Danielle, what's up?" he asks.

"Are you with Nicole?" I demand, getting straight to the point.

"No," he shakes his head. "We're just friends. Why? She'd have told you if I was going out with her, anyway."

"I was just wondering," I shrug, trying to act like I don't care, really, I'm just enquiring . . . when in reality the thought of the two of them together is driving me insane. "You're spending a lot of time with her. You two act like you're together."

"Not that much time. I just like talking to her. She's nice."

"Do you fancy her?"

He grins. "Does it matter?"

"You *do*," I smile. Keep up the smile, act like you don't care, like the two of you are just friends.

"She's a friend," he says.

"Sure," I roll my eyes.

"Besides, if I say anything, I know you'll tell her," he adds.

"I wouldn't. Honestly." Under normal circumstances I would, yes. Not now. I'd lie blatantly. ("Nicole, I was talking to Mark and he says he's not interested in you one bit. So I guess I'm just going to have to have him.")

"You would," he insists. "So even if I did like her, I wouldn't tell you."

"Don't you trust me?" Cue pout.

"About as far as I can throw you," he jokes. At least, he'd better be joking, or else we'll all be finding out how far *I* can throw *him*.

"Mark, I'm hurt," I feign devastation.

"Want me to kiss it all better?" he asks.

"Yes," I say in a little-girl voice.

I think he might actually do it, too, until Liz and Tara come over to talk to us, and the moment is ruined. Sigh.

Eric comes back into school on Thursday, which interrupts the daily tedium as we get to ask him how his summer was and he gets to tell us long, drawn-out stories. In the middle of one anecdote, he looks across the classroom at Naomi and Caitlin somewhat longingly, then continues talking. I wonder if he still likes Caitlin. They used to go out – they broke up in June, right after the exams ended. Her idea, although now she regrets it, as she told us. She still likes him but is convinced he hates her now. Which is why the two of them are over there ignoring Eric. I debate going over and then decide that since this way I get to be near Mark, I'll stay over here. Besides, I can count the number of times I saw Eric over the summer on one hand, and it was usually just when we were calling around for Michelle. ("We" being me, Rachel and Naomi, because Caitlin was studiously avoiding her ex-boyfriend. Rachel's an ex of his, too, but I guess she's over it by now – plus she's always so good at coping with these things.) So I stay, and pretend to listen to Eric when I'm really gazing at Mark.

How could he have wanted to break up with me, anyway? I mean, I thought everything was going fine. I was happy. I assumed he was, too. Was it just that he was bored with me? Fed up because we'd been together for so long? If that was the reason, then maybe what we need is space, followed by an emotional and long-anticipated reunion. (Well, we have the space part. When do we get to the good stuff?)

Maybe – gasp – he was actually telling the truth when he dumped (such an ugly word, but it fully expresses its uglier meaning) me, and really does believe we're better as friends. That theory, however, has several flaws. Number one – why on earth would any normal teenage boy tell the truth about a break-up? Why would they do that? They make excuses. It's a fact of life. Number two – we aren't friends any more, not the way we used to be. I can't talk to him the way I used to, even before we were together.

Maybe he really hates me and wants to cut me out of his life completely. Now *that's* a depressing thought.

It's also the one that sticks in my mind and taunts me for the rest of the day.

"Rache, wait for me, will you?" I ask at the end of the day. She has a habit of heading home before me. I don't know why. She zooms out the door the second the last bell goes. Maybe she's trying to get some studying done. For the Leaving. I wouldn't be surprised.

"Sure," she shrugs, looking almost annoyed that I asked her. She taps her foot as she waits and drums her fingers on the locker next to mine as I shove books in there and pull on my jacket.

"Why are you in such a rush, anyway?" I ask as we walk out of there.

"I'm not. I just . . . don't want to hang around in school any longer than I have to," she explains. "I just want to get home."

We spend the walk home bitching about our teachers. Well, I bitch, and Rachel defends their actions. According to her, teachers are good people, really. If you ask me, they're evil monsters who devote their entire time to making our lives hell. Then again, teachers *like* Rachel. She's Mature and Responsible and Diligent and Intelligent and all those other good things. Total teacher's pet.

I remember this one time when we were in primary school, out in the yard at breaktime, and a couple of us got into a fight. I don't even remember what it was about, now, but I know that Rachel and myself participated. And the teacher on yard duty came over and started giving out to me and Tara, my best friend at the time, and completely ignored the fact that Rachel had been involved at all. People always make exceptions for her, because she's so wonderful.

Sometimes I really hate her guts.

When we get in, Rachel goes up to her bedroom and turns on the music. I listen for a moment. It's the depressing, emotionally-wrenching type. Again. I debate – to go in or not to go in? To ask Rachel what the hell is up with her and why is she being so weird lately, or to leave it?

Then I remember that it's *Rachel*. The girl who has everything under control and doesn't need the help of her less organised older sister (who has yet to get over her ex-boyfriend, for God's sake!). Suddenly I feel pretty pathetic. Rachel's got the brains and beauty, she's got Adam wrapped around her little finger, and everyone loves her. Meanwhile, I certainly don't have brains, and as for beauty, I'm not so sure about that at all. Mark is too busy adoring Nicole to realise that I still like him, although that's probably a good thing. There's something so hopeless and sad about not being able to accept the end of a relationship.

So, I decide as I open the door to my own room, the last thing Rachel needs is advice from a loser like me.

I wonder if she'll let me borrow those CDs of hers. They seem to match my mood.

Part Two

Results

11

Nicole

Wednesday, 18th September. The day of judgement. The day of reckoning. The biggest day in our entire lives, so far. The day we . . . (drumroll, please) get our Junior Cert results.

On this highly important day, I show how much I care by being late to school. It's ten past nine by the time I get into class. I get yelled at by Mr Traynor, our rather demented vice-principal, on the way in, and ignore him. Just because he's stuck in a dead-end job that he clearly hates doesn't mean he has to take it out on us, the innocent victims of his wrath.

It's not like we're doing anything important in school, anyway. Most of us are totally hyped up and they know the chances of us learning anything are slim to none. There's no one who can actually concentrate. Some people can't wait to see how they did; the rest of us just want to get them so we can go out and celebrate.

I'm a big fan of celebrating, myself. Grades? Oh, right, yeah. Whatever.

Anyway, the teachers are letting us watch a video. We've got Miss Morgan supervising us for one of the classes and she looks like she's going to have a heart attack when we start getting noisy. Poor thing. She's just not able to handle the class, and I swear, one of these days she'll break down in tears in front of all of us and then go home and retire to bed with a nervous breakdown, turn into an alcoholic and never teach ever again. So far I've been trying to avert this possibility by getting most of our crowd to shut up and stop messing whenever it looks like we're getting close to driving her over the edge.

By eleven-thirty I have to admit I'm as excited about the results as, say, Grace, who *knows* she'll get all Honours, or Mark, who has never failed anything in his life. Of course, both of them are going around convinced that they'll get NGs in everything, and the rest of us are rolling our eyes and joining in with the "I'm going to do worse than you" game.

Danielle: "Well, I didn't open one book for the entire year, so I'm *definitely* going to fail."

Caitlin: "Yeah, but you paid attention in class. I didn't. I'm *so* going to fail."

Sean: "Yeah, right! None of you are going to fail. You're all brainy, not thick like me."

And on and on and on . . .

My parents don't really mind how I do. I mean, they'd like to me to do well, but if I don't, they won't really care. I wonder if that's the best way to have it. Rachel and Caitlin are under pressure to do brilliantly; while Danielle and

Naomi are practically expected to get crap results. It's unbelievable how much our parents screw up our lives. As the hour draws closer, Caitlin's a nervous wreck and Naomi is praying she'll do well to prove her dad wrong.

I text Rachel, who's not in school today but will be heading over to her old school to get her results later on. As expected, she's panic-stricken. Her text messages, however, are still as grammatically and punctuationally correct as they always are. She hasn't lost her mind just yet.

At twelve o'clock, we get our results, in these white envelopes with our full names printed on the outside.

"*Francesca?*" says Adam incredulously, looking at my middle name.

"I know," I groan. I still haven't forgiven my parents for that one. It's such an *old-person's* name.

I open the envelope to find a little cream slip with all the subjects listed on it, in Irish. God. They torture us further by giving us information in a language none of us understand.

I get three As – in pass Maths, pass Science, and CSPE. Bs in Art and Home Ec. Cs in Irish (what, I didn't fail it?) and Geography. Ds in History, English and French. Hey, look at me, I passed everything! Go me!

It's chaos everywhere – the whole of TY is running around screaming and hugging and smiling and comparing. "How'd you do? How'd you do?"

Everyone seems to have done better than they expected – or, should I say, better than they *said* they expected. You can tell Naomi's pissed off that she got a C in Art, but since she was saying earlier that she'd probably failed (waiting to hear reassurances of "Of course you won't. You're *deadly* at Art!") she can hardly complain.

People who did really well give their results in grades; everyone else says how many honours and passes and fails they got. Like Grace with her four As, five Bs and a C (how the *hell* can she be that smart?) or Mark with his five As, five Bs. The rest of us gape at them in shock.

While everyone is still finding out how everyone else did – saying "Oh my God, well done!" and meaning it when it's a good result and saying it but not with much sincerity to someone who did terribly but who you don't want to feel bad about it – I ring Rachel on her mobile. Miss Morgan passes by and I worry for a second that she'll give out to me for having a phone, but all she does is ask me how I did, and then say "Well done!" (I should have known not to worry – I don't think she's capable of giving out to someone.)

The phone rings and finally Rache answers. "Hello?"

"Heya! How'd you do?"

"All right," she says, sounding strangely tense. "How about you?"

"Three As – but two of them in pass, two Bs, two Cs, and three Ds. I passed everything, can you believe it?" I laugh.

"Well done!" Still tense. Oh God, please let her have got the results she wants, please, please, please.

"Are you okay?" I ask.

"Yeah, I'm fine," she says hollowly.

"Come on, how'd you do?"

"Nine As and a B."

"OH MY GOD!" I scream, so loudly that half the year turns around to look at me. Danielle and Caitlin rush over.

"Rache, that's brilliant! Oh my God, I can't believe you did so well!" I exclaim.

She doesn't say anything.

"You're happy with that, right?" I ask.

"Yeah, of course," she says, but I know that if I could see her she'd be shrugging. No, she's not, I suddenly realise.

I don't understand why. I mean, I do, in a way. She could have done better, so she's not happy. But she got fantastic results! If I had her results I'd throw a party. In Hawaii. And invite everyone I knew. That's how happy I'd be. But she's not.

"You want to talk to Danielle?" I ask, and hand the phone over to her sister.

"How'd she do?" Caitlin asks.

"Nine As, one B," I inform her.

Caitlin looks like she's going to faint. "Okay. I *was* happy with what I got until you told me that!" she finally says, but she's grinning. That's the difference between her and Rachel. For Caitlin, someone else's success doesn't diminish her own, but for Rache, the thought of someone doing better than her suddenly makes her bad. Caitlin has to do well, Rachel has to be the best.

It's so messed up. I don't want Rachel to feel bad, but I

don't know how I can make her feel better, if she refuses to accept the fact that she has actually done really well, even though she hasn't got ten As. Who *gets* ten As, anyway? Who puts *that* much work into it? Who cares so much about their results that they work *that* hard to get them?

Rachel, that's who, I sigh.

12

Rachel

"Congratulations, Rache! I *knew* you'd do brilliantly!" Danielle enthuses via mobile, her tone identical to Nicole's. I know to them my results are great, but they don't get it. They can be delighted with their Bs and Cs and Ds, but I'm not one of those people who can settle for being average, or *quite* good.

I got nine As and a B. The B was in Irish. That hateful B, tainting the slip of paper with its presence. It was like – okay, how can I explain it so you'll understand? Say you're on this fantastic holiday. It's perfect – sun, sea, sand, boys. You've been looking forward to this holiday for ages, and you wish it didn't have to end. Then you find out that your worst enemy is coming along with you. Some easy-going people would deal with it and not let it spoil their fun. Most people, however, would freak out and find that their holiday was ruined by this person being there. Sure, everything *else* was perfect, but you still had to deal with someone you hated.

That B was the worst enemy who'd wound up staying in the room next door, who called around every morning wanting to know what we were doing today. The sensible thing would be to not let it destroy my holiday, but I'm not exactly feeling sensible at the moment.

I mean, I *worked*. I studied and I memorised and I practised. And then I went in and did the exams and even though there were some hard questions, I thought and hoped I'd do as well as I wanted.

And now this. A B.

I remember in *Smash Hits* years and years ago – okay, I was probably about ten or so – there was this interview with some band, and they were asked how they felt about getting to number two. And they said that it didn't make any difference whether they were at number two or number forty – the point was, they hadn't got to number one. They hadn't reached the top.

Danielle read it and rolled her eyes, thinking they were crazy, and that if she was a pop star she wouldn't be complaining if she got to number two. But I understood completely. It's how I feel now. I could have failed and I'd feel the exact same way as I do now. I didn't get the top result. I didn't get ten As. I could have done better.

Ciara Maloney is rushing around hugging everyone like crazy and asking them how they did. She says "Well done!" with a big smile, and then waits for you to ask her how she did.

At which point she'll say, oh-so-modestly (oh *please*,

does the girl have a humble bone in her body?) that she got ten As.

I might have been able to cope with my nine As and one B if it had been the best in my year. Then it still would have been slightly satisfying.

I hate Ciara Maloney with a fiery passion. I imagine stabbing her repeatedly with a really, really big knife.

I hate the girls from my old class pretending they're so glad to see me and then drifting off without saying goodbye. A couple of weeks without me and they've already forgotten me. Julie hugs me and then goes off with Lauren. Since when are they even friends? As far as I knew they were officially cordial but unofficially didn't get on *at all*. A lot of things have changed. Siobhán is now friends with Katherine and Orla. Brenda, who used to be reasonably friendly, has turned into a bitch, while Clodagh, formerly my worst nightmare, is full of smiles and is probably the most sincere person I talk to.

It's official. I'm an outsider. Okay, I've always been an outsider, but it's never been as pronounced as this. I don't fit in here. I don't fit in at my new school.

I honestly don't want to think to myself something as pathetic and clichéd as "Nobody loves me!" but it really does feel like that.

Mum is waiting in the car for me. The first thing she asks, is, naturally enough, "Well, how did you get on?"

"Nine As, one B," I say. By this stage I'm used to saying it and can even make myself sound happy with this result.

She's pleased. I'm stunned. I didn't think she'd be happy with anything less than perfection.

I almost want to ask, "Aren't you disappointed I didn't get ten As?" but I don't want to risk it. I'm scared of what she'll say.

But she doesn't seem like she minds that I got one B.

But I still do.

Time to face facts, Rache. Mum and Dad do put pressure on me. But it's nothing compared to the pressure I put myself under. I'm the one who has lately been basing her opinion of herself on two things only – weight and grades.

I know neither of them are meant to matter that much. Logically I know that a B is a good grade and that I'm an above-average, some might even say great, student. Logically I know that I shouldn't be worrying so much about my weight and that real friends don't judge you by what you look like but by who you are.

The question is, who is Rachel Connolly? I'm a girl who obsesses over grades and her weight, going over the top for both of them. But apart from that, who am I? I don't know. I just don't know, and that's why I can't stop. That's why I have to keep focussing on the things that I do know about and can work on and can feel in control of in some tiny little way.

I can feel myself panicking – adrenaline pumping, heart pounding. I don't know why I feel so scared. I want to get out of the car, but we're still not home. I wait, thinking of all the methods you can use to calm yourself down. I try counting to ten but I just speed through it, onetwothreefourfivesixseveneightninten without stopping. I leap out of the car as soon as Mum pulls up in the driveway, my keys already out so I can open the door. Even now I realise it's important to keep up a front, try not to act suspiciously, in case Mum figures out something's going on. She can't know. She can't.

Once it's done I think I should be okay. Now that I've thrown up I should feel better, the way you do when you're sick. I guess it doesn't work when it's self-induced vomiting. I wonder manically am I doing the right thing. Statistics and definitions swirl around in my head mixed in with the advice from *Sugar's* problem page. Eating disorder. Bulimia. They're bad, I know that much. I'm not stupid. But I've always thought that I'm not like the girls who write into those pages. I can stop any time I want to, and anyway, it's all over-hyped anyway. It can't be that harmful for you. They just want to scare you. They want to stop you from doing anything that's out of the ordinary.

Maybe if they tried it they'd understand why it works. It's the sensible thing when you consider the alternatives. Eat what you want and get fat; deprive yourself of food and you get thin. This way *works*. At least it should. I haven't lost that much weight yet but I guess that's because I'm not making myself sick enough. Maybe I'm messing things up by not eating sometimes. I don't know. But my plan should work. Eventually.

By this stage I feel more relaxed, almost soothed. I'm in control, I don't have a problem, I'm going to get thin and then everything's going to be okay. I can feel it.

13

Danielle

Of all the people I'd have expected, *Michelle* is the one to ask "Do I look fat in this?"

"What?" Naomi asks in disbelief, turning away from her own mirror and staring at Michelle. "Yeah, Michelle, you look fat. The way Calista Flockhart does."

Michelle grins. "You're too kind."

Naomi grins back. "No problem."

I watch this little exchange, reminded of Nicole's current opinion of Naomi. I'm getting paranoid, I know. I was the one who spent most of the summer hanging around with Naomi, yet I'm letting one of Nicole's theories turn me into Little Miss Suspicious. I don't know what the big deal is. I don't give a crap if she's a lesbian. She's just – you know, Naomi, the friend who knows how to cheer you up when you're depressed and who looks like butter wouldn't melt in her now-coated-with-red-lipstick mouth.

So stop acting so judgemental and get back to the important things in life, I tell myself, and return to the important task of applying makeup.

Crazy as it may seem, *my mother* – yes, that's right, my mother – is letting a couple of my friends sleep over at our house tonight. After we got back. Rache and I spent about two seconds deciding on Caitlin, Michelle, Naomi and Nicole. Well, the first three names were no problem. She suggested Nicole and I agreed, reluctantly. I'm still a little wary of Nicole and not sure what the hell is going on with her and Mark, but she's still a good friend. Besides, in the huge emotional upheaval of getting our results, I was feeling glad to have her as a friend.

Of course, in that strange, happy state I even hugged *Marian*. Who is Marian? Good question. We were friends in first year, had a big fight, I went home and cried for a couple of hours, and then went in the next day determined to hate her for the rest of my life. By the end of the week it had dulled to a vague hatred, by the end of the year a mild dislike, and I wouldn't have even remembered that fight if she hadn't brought it up jokingly in Spanish one day.

My point is . . . well, my point has long since jumped out the window and driven away, leaving a trail of dust behind. But I was trying to say that the weird sense of joy that accompanies good news (like not failing any subjects in your Junior Cert) temporarily displaces your sense of reason.

So now I'm not so sure how happy I am that Nicole's

sleeping over tonight, but I doubt I'll be sober enough to care by the time we get home.

By the time we get into town Nicole is completely and utterly pissed. I suspect she drank even before she came down to our house. The rest of us are fine, waiting until later – Naomi has vodka in her bag, in a Sprite bottle, which will no doubt be empty by the end of the night when we've all had more.

I don't feel like drinking much, which is weird because I've never agreed with Nicole's "You don't need alcohol to have a good time" policy. Ironic now that she's the one who appears to be needing an awful lot of it.

Caitlin leads the way, being the best with directions and being the only one who really knows where she's going. (Having a bad sense of direction runs in my family. Rachel, my dad and I are hopeless – my mum is the one who understands maps and somehow seems to instinctively know which turn to take.)

When we get inside it's packed. I see a few people from school and there's a couple I recognise from other schools. Even though it's a Junior Cert students' thing, there are a few older guys hanging around. Not older as in sixty-year-old men leering after fifteen-year-olds. Older as in they've probably left school by now. Still a little weird, but not as creepy.

Naomi's the first to be asked to meet someone. We've been there barely five minutes. She refuses, not making a big deal of it but firmly letting the friend of the guy know she's not interested. I glance over at Nicole, expecting her to be trying to make eye contact with me so she can look pointedly at me, but she's distracted, barely paying attention to what's going on.

Rachel, Michelle and Caitlin are throwing themselves into the dancing, just having fun. I wish I could be like that, but I'm too concerned about looking out for people (Mark) and wondering how I look. Naomi and Nicole are off talking to some of our friends, and eventually I give up trying to stay perfect and just have a good time. I love dancing, anyway.

Adam, Mark and Donal show up after a while and manoeuvre their way towards us. I can feel my heart pounding already, and all he's doing is standing there.

"Where's Rachel?" Mark wants to know, yelling over the music.

He wants Rachel. Typical. I look around for her, blinking back tears.

"She's gone to the toilet, I think," Michelle volunteers. Her words do, naturally, have to be repeated about a zillion times before Mark can hear her.

It transpires that it's Adam, and not Mark, that wants to meet Rachel, and for that I'm relieved. Even if I still have trouble accepting the fact that this is my little sister they're talking about and that in my head she's too innocent to be meeting anyone.

I tell the boys that I'll go talk to her, and push through the crowds. The toilets downstairs are crammed with girls a) drinking, b) crying or c) doing their make-up. But no Rache. I try upstairs. There isn't much of an upstairs – the stairs is sort of hidden away and when you go up them there's just a couple of storerooms, clearly somewhere no one's meant to go or would want to go – but I do find another toilet.

I can hear puking sounds when I go in, and I'm not surprised. Usually by this stage you have some people feeling sick after drinking, and it gets worse as the night goes on. However, there's only one stall occupied, so I'm guessing it has to be Rache. I didn't realise she'd had that much to drink, I muse. She's not the world's most hardened drinker, but it takes a lot to get her throwing up.

I'm about to call out her name, just to check, when I hear the toilet flush. She walks out, looking weirdly healthy for someone who's just been throwing up. There's just something wrong about this. It feels weird. She doesn't seem sick. She's not acting like someone who is. And the second she sees me, she jumps, guiltily.

No way, I think, but a scary thought is beginning to grow in my mind.

"Hey! You scared me," she smiles.

"You okay?" I ask.

"Me? Oh, yeah . . . just too much to drink, I guess."

"You don't look that sick," I can't help but comment.

She pauses for a second too long. "I suppose I've just gotten it out of my system, you know? Why'd you come up here, anyway?"

Nice casual changing-of-the-subject, Rache.

"I was looking for you. Adam wants to meet you," I inform her.

She looks at me in disbelief. "Yeah, right."

"Seriously," I say, wondering how she has so little self-esteem. Has she forgotten she's the better sister or something?

She shrugs. "Yeah, well, I still feel a bit sick. I don't feel up to it."

"Rache?" I say softly.

"Yeah?" She looks straight at me.

"Are you okay? Seriously, like? Are you really okay?" I want to scream "Why are you lying to me and what's really going on?" but I hold back.

She glances away, and I can see an expression of relief flit across her face. But then it disappears and she's got the mask on again.

"Everything's okay. Really," she smiles. Falsely. Lying to me.

"Because if it's not, you can tell me. You know you can."

"I'm *fine*, Danielle," she says, sounding almost irritated.

Maybe she is. Maybe I'm overreacting. Maybe everything really is okay and tomorrow I'll laugh at the fact that I was so worried about her.

Maybe not.

14

Nicole

I had a huge fight with my parents when I got home. It was about time. We hadn't fought viciously in weeks – we were overdue for an argument. They love finding things to criticise about me.

When I gave them my results they were happy enough, but then they had to bring up tonight. Babbling on about how they hoped I'd be responsible and not drink and so on and so forth. It was mostly Don'ts, as their little talks so often are. Don't drink. Don't do drugs. Don't get pregnant. The one thing they never lecture me about is not to smoke. One, because I don't – I hate it with a passion, because of reason number two – they smoke. Like chimneys. It drives me crazy. I hate them for smoking.

The one thing I remember most vividly about primary school is watching a video about why we shouldn't smoke, and it showed those blackened smokers' lungs. And the nine-year-old Nicole went home and cried herself to sleep and worried for months that any day now her parents were going to drop dead because they smoked so much.

Amazing what can get through to you when you're a kid. Anyway, I brought up the fact that they did smoke to them today, saying that they were hardly in a position to lecture me about my habits, and then mentioned the tiny little fact that my dad had a kid before he was married, so obviously premarital sex wasn't frowned upon in our family . . .

And so on. It wound up with a whole lot of name-calling and me storming out of the house with my overnight bag. I went over to Mark's house. His mum was out and the two of us had a bit to drink. I needed to. I had to take my mind off family crap. Then I said I had to get over to the Connollys and he said he'd see me later.

So far I haven't seen him, because I'm making my way over to where Niall is. He showed up tonight with a couple of his friends. I don't know what they're doing here – or maybe I do. Maybe he's here for me.

He looks surprised to see me, but pleased, which is a relief. He suggests we go outside and I agree.

I'm not sure why I approached him but I know that I had to. Once I saw him I couldn't just ignore him.

Now he seems to have forgotten about what happened before. His girlfriend isn't here. They must've broken up. Good.

He likes me. He's been drinking, of course, but I know it's not just the alcohol talking and that he really does like me.

He's showing me just how much he does.

But then it starts to feel weird and wrong and scary and I want him to stop. Get away from me, I want to say, but the words won't come out.

No one's around. I'm terrified. It's now that I realise my greatest fear is not of, as I thought, murder, but rape. I'm praying to a deity I've ignored for years in the hope that I'll be rescued.

The word "rescued" rolling around in my mind stuns me into some kind of weird rage. Rescued implies being a victim, and Nicole Robinson doesn't "do" being a victim, thank you very much.

It's very clichéd, I have to admit, but kneeing him where it hurts seems to do the job, stunning him momentarily, and I race back inside, shaking.

I see Mark. He suddenly seems so much more attractive. Maybe I've been in love with him all along, I decide. He approaches me and I smile at him.

And then I kiss him softly on the cheek, then lightly moving down to his lips. My Mark. He's the one I really want, I realise. Our friendship has just been a temporary situation until we both admitted how we felt about one another.

This is it. True Love. The real kind. Not like Niall. This is something special. I love him.

15

Rachel

She knows something's up, but I don't think she's figured out just quite what it is yet. For a second, I thought about telling her everything. She's my sister. She can be a bitch at times, but at the end of the day, she cares. If I told her maybe it'd help. Keeping everything a secret is getting so hard. I've thought about confiding in Nicole or Caitlin, especially in my more panicked what-am-I-really-doing-to-myself moments, but I always stop myself.

I'm scared of telling them, of how they'll react. I'm scared that they'll think it's disgusting. I'm even more scared that they'll think it's none of their business because they don't really want to be friends with me, anyway.

And it's for that same reason that I didn't tell Danielle anything. Because I know that she's just like everyone else. They act concerned but they really don't want to hear about your problems. They're just being polite.

"I'm going to go talk to him," Danielle decides.

"Seriously?" Michelle asks. "Because if you go talk to him, you'll end up either meeting him, or being rejected."

"Yeah, well, I'm hoping for option number one," she grins, although her smile is hiding her nervousness.

"Good luck," Michelle says, and I echo the sentiment. Danielle turns to make her way over to him, then stops.

Puzzled, I look over.

Mark is meeting someone. Someone who looks very familiar. Someone who answers to the name of Nicole.

Danielle stares at them for a few minutes, transfixed, before she turns back around to us. Her face makes me want to cry. There's hurt and anger and pain etched across it.

Michelle looks at her sympathetically. "I'm sorry."

I reach out to touch her arm. "Yeah, me too."

She takes a deep breath. "Oh, well, it's no big deal, right? I mean, I'm not going out with him or anything, anyway, you know?"

It's only when Michelle hugs her that she starts crying.

I wish I was as good as Michelle is in these situations. She seems to know exactly what to say and what to do, whereas I feel useless. I'm still pretty shocked by Nicole meeting Mark. She knows how Danielle feels about him. Maybe she's drunk, but that's no excuse. And he – well, I can't really fault him, I suppose. It *is* sort of tacky to meet your ex-girlfriend's friend, but it's not like he's never done it before, and he and Danielle split up ages ago, anyway.

Or maybe I just have a soft spot for Mark because we once went out and he was my first real boyfriend.

Either way, what I think doesn't really matter and isn't going to help Danielle feel better, is it?

We get the Nitelink bus back home. There's quite a few of us from our area, Nicole and Mark included, looking very cosy – and very pissed. Nicole gets off at our stop and joins us.

"What are you doing here?" Danielle demands.

She looks confused. "I'm staying here, remember? My stuff's in here . . . you asked me to sleep over, remember?"

"Yeah, I remember. Do you remember that you spent the whole night cuddled up to Mark? You *know* I like him, Nicole. You *know* I do. And you just went off with him anyway! So don't think you can just come back to my house now and act like nothing happened."

Nicole's upset. "But I didn't think – I can't go home, Danielle." Of course she can't. Her parents will kill her if she comes in while in a state like she is now.

"So sleep on the streets," Danielle snaps. "It's what you deserve, you stupid slut!"

I can't believe what I'm hearing. They've been friends forever, and had more than their share of fights, but I've never heard this level of coldness coming from my sister.

"Guys, just calm down, okay?" Caitlin tries to soothe, being mindful that it is the middle of the night and that we're out on the road fighting.

"Caitlin, stay out of this!" Danielle snaps.

"Oh, typical, take your problems out on everyone else," Nicole says. "Just because you can't *handle* the fact that

Mark doesn't want to go out with you any more . . . God, I wonder why? Is it because you're ugly, or boring, or *both?*"

"Look who's talking! At least I'm not a little slut like you are."

"That's a nice way of saying that you can't get a fella, is it?"

"You're the one who had to go steal someone else's guy, so don't look at me!"

"He's not yours! You don't own him. Deal with the fact that he dumped you."

Danielle looks like she's been hit, and then I realise. She's always given off the impression that their split was a mutual agreement. We thought it might have been him who ended it, but we never actually said it. Until Nicole.

"Stop fighting, would you?" Naomi sighs. "You're going to wake up half of Dublin if you keep this up."

"Shut up, Naomi." This time it's Nicole's turn to snap.

"Why don't you shut up?" Naomi isn't as easily put off as Caitlin was.

Nicole smirks. "'Cause I'm not a lezzer, that's why."

"That's *way* out of line, Nicole," Michelle steps in, glancing at Naomi whose angelic face is pale.

"Oh, I see we've got two of them on our hands! Honestly, isn't *anyone* straight these days? Although, personally, Michelle, I just wrote you off as frigid. Please forgive me for my assumption. It won't happen again."

"You little bitch," Michelle mutters.

"Oh, Little Miss Perfect *can* actually insult people!" Nicole sneered. "Although you're going to have to come up with something better than that to hurt my feelings. My mum uses it so often it's lost all meaning."

"It certainly suits you," Danielle mutters.

Before they get into another heated row, I firmly step in before someone says something else I know they'll regret in the morning. With a sense of confidence that seems to have appeared out of nowhere, I say, "Okay. Listen. You two can fight out on the streets like a couple of knackers until dawn, but I'm going back to the house. Come on, guys. Let's go."

Setting off at a brisk pace for my house, I don't even look back to see who's following until I reach the door. They're all on their way, having silently fallen into step with me. I unlock the door and hold it open until everyone's inside, watching them as they go through.

The original plan was for all of us to sleep downstairs in the living-room. I quickly realise it's not a good idea.

"Nicole, Caitlin, bring your sleeping bags up to my room, will you? Naomi and Michelle, you can take yours up to Danielle's," I direct.

They all move quietly. No one wants to talk. Everyone's scared of getting yelled at by Nicole, except me. There's nothing she can say about me that I haven't already thought about myself. Besides, this is my house. She's already *persona non grata* with Danielle, so if she wants to sleep over she'll stay on good terms with me.

The silence lasts even when the three of us are getting ready for bed in my room. I can hear conversation and crying from Danielle's room, but it's quiet in here. Maybe Nicole's ashamed of what's she said, or angry, or whatever, but it's keeping her from talking, and for that I'm grateful. The person I know as one of my best friends was a horrible person tonight, and I don't think I could talk to her civilly right now.

Caitlin is scared to speak, too. I catch her eye and smile reassuringly at her, acknowledging the tension.

I close my eyes and try to forget about everything, hoping that sleep will come soon.

16

Danielle

Fights with any of my friends, in particular Nicole, tend to take a lot out of me, but this is ridiculous. I'm shaking. My eyes keep filling up with tears.

It's just too much. I'm worried about Rachel and then Nicole goes and meets Mark and acts like it's not a big deal and insults me, and on top of it all is still in this house, probably trying to win Rache and Caitlin over to her side.

Michelle and Naomi are upset as well. There's a whole lot of crying and hugging going on, and after a few minutes I just start laughing hysterically. They join in, and eventually we calm down.

"I still can't believe she did it, though," Michelle says.

"Which part?" Naomi asks bitterly. Exactly what I was thinking.

"Everything! I mean, I always thought she was so nice – but God, she was a total and utter bitch tonight. The things she said! Come on, Naomi. She wasn't exactly friendly to you either."

"Yeah, well, at least she was just talking shit about you. She pretty much hit the nail on the head as far as I'm concerned," Naomi mutters.

I inhale sharply, but Michelle doesn't miss a beat. "Even so, there was no way for her to be so – I don't know – derogatory." (Big word. Where's Rache when you need her?) "I mean, she acts like she's got the right to judge everyone. It just pisses me off."

"You're not the only one," I say.

It's official. We have moved on from Sadness to Anger. We express our opinions of Nicole with vehemence and hatred, using lots of cursing to fully get our point across. Incidents from the past are dredged up and bitched about.

Once I get into it, it's actually quite fun. But then I start thinking about her and Mark, and I sink into depression again.

I'm awake earlier than usual the following morning, and go downstairs for breakfast. Rachel's already there, sipping coffee.

"Heya," she says.

"Hey. Are the others awake yet?"

"Nah. Not yet. How about your room?"

"They're still asleep. Probably exhausted from all the talking we did last night."

"We heard you," Rachel nods.

"How much did you hear?" I say cautiously. If Nicole

heard us talking about her, it's not going to be pretty, although she's the type that would have walked in last night and picked another fight if she had heard.

"Nothing, really," she reassures. "It was really muffled, we just knew that you guys were talking. And we weren't. The tension! Unbelievable. None of us said anything all night."

"Oh. I though maybe Nicole would've brainwashed you into taking her side," I say lightly.

She laughs. "Yeah. Right. After what she did last night, are you kidding?"

"I wasn't exactly a saint myself," I remind her.

"Compared to her you were."

I have to admit that I was thinking that myself.

"She might've been right about some stuff, though," I say, thinking of what she said about needing to deal with Mark not wanting to be with me any more.

"About Mark?"

"Yeah."

"She could've been nicer about the way she said it, though. And she was probably just saying it so that she doesn't have to feel guilty about meeting him when she knows you still like him," Rachel says matter-of-factly.

I smile.

"What?" she demands.

"You're so good at making me feel better," I grin. "Thanks."

She rolls her eyes, but looks pleased.

"How's Naomi doing?" she asks.

"She's mad at herself for the way she reacted to Nicole. She thinks she should have handled it better instead of going all quiet, because it's fairly obvious that she only shut up because she couldn't exactly argue with what Nicole said, you know?"

Rachel nods. "Yeah, but – we're her friends. It's not like we're going to turn against her or anything."

"She's insecure, I suppose," I say. "Michelle's pretty upset, too."

"Nicole wasn't exactly the nicest to her, either, was she?" Rache sighs.

"Yeah, but once again, she was scarily accurate. Brian had said the same thing to her a couple of hours beforehand, so Michelle's starting to worry that she's abnormal or something."

Rachel grins. "I wouldn't worry about what Brian says. He's a total sex maniac."

"I've noticed. He's not exactly my type, either, but she seems to like him. Anyway, he got pissed off because she wouldn't do anything more than meet. He wanted a . . . big hug," I finish rapidly as Mum enters the kitchen.

"It's nice that young men are so undemanding these days," she says.

Is it just me or is she becoming less uptight lately? Before we know it, she'll be normal.

"Have a good time last night?" she enquires.

"All right," Rachel answers. "It was fun, but there was a bit of drama as well – you know how it is."

Mum nods, eyeing each of us, noting that neither of us

appears to be hung over. She seems almost disappointed that she can't lecture us on the evils of alcohol.

"Your friends made an awful lot of noise coming in last night," she comments.

Knew it. I knew she'd have to get at us about *something*.

"Did we wake you up?" Rachel, the good daughter, asks. The bad daughter doesn't care.

"I was just drifting off when you came back," she says. "You were all fairly late back, too."

"The bus," Rache explains.

Mum nods. Pauses. Then starts up again. "When do you have to be in school?"

"We have to be in at eleven, but Michelle's starting at the usual time," Rachel speaks up once more. She finishes her coffee. I gulp down a cup of tea. We leave. I suppose it's terrible that we're so eager to get away from our own mother, but if she was yours – well, you'd understand.

17

Nicole

The moment I wake up the throbbing headache and overwhelming nausea hit me, quickly followed by the realisation that I'm not in my own house, I'm in the Connollys', which reminds me of –

Oh, crap.

It's not the first time I've had memories of the previous night flooding back to me in a horrible rush like this, but I've never been as incredibly bitchy as I was last night.

Mark!

Double crap.

I'm not interested in Mark. There's no way I'm interested in Mark. He's like a brother. He's my tell-all-my-problems-to guy. I can't go out with him!

Or meet him – oh, wait, too late for that, Nic! You really made a mess of things, didn't you?

I want to curl up into a little ball and die. I mean, *die*. If I had anything sharp with me I'd be busy slitting my wrists, but as it is I'm just slithering as far inside my sleeping bag as I can go, hoping that I'll find a conveniently-located black hole in there somewhere.

Nope. No black holes. No earthquakes tearing up the house, either. No raging fires to burn me alive. I'm still here.

Why oh why oh why was I so horrible last night? Apart from the obvious reasons, I mean. Like the fight with my parents or the fact that I was locked or the matter of Niall? Not to mention Danielle's possessiveness of Mark. That was what set it off, I suppose. Especially because last night I thought – well, I thought that I fancied him. Which I don't. No way. He's lovely, he really is, but as a boyfriend? I can't see it, mostly because he knows way too much about me already, and I'm better off with him as a friend.

Oh My God.

Why won't this all go away? Why isn't it disappearing? Why am I still trapped in this horrible universe where I've done bad, stupid things and everyone probably hates me now (oh, God, I'm remembering what I said to Naomi and Michelle who are never, ever, ever going to speak to me again) except of course Mark who probably thinks that I've been secretly lusting after him for ages.

It's only a quarter past eight. Maybe I can sneak out without them seeing me. Everyone else is probably still asleep. I take a peek outside. Rachel's gone, but Caitlin's still sleeping, her eyes closed and her hair everywhere. I wonder whether it's safe to get dressed and then quietly slip outside when I hear voices and footsteps coming up the stairs. Rachel and Danielle.

"Do you think they're up yet?" Rachel asks.

"Michelle probably is," Danielle says, "since she has to get to school for what? Quarter to nine?"

"Mmm," Rachel confirms. I can hear a door opening, and I instantly feign sleep, but after a few moments I realise that they've both gone into Danielle's room.

Rachel probably wants to avoid me too, I realise. Sure, she was nice last night. Well, she didn't kick me out, at any rate, and let me sleep in her room. But she's known Michelle for ages, so obviously she's going to take her side, plus Danielle's her sister. I have to admit to feeling hurt, and jealous of Michelle. I want Rachel to take my side. I want *anyone* to take my side, admittedly, but I thought she was one of my best friends. And even last night, in the state I was in, I wasn't able to bring myself to say anything bitchy to her. She's just way too sweet. Suddenly I feel like crying.

I start getting dressed in the clothes I was wearing last night. Originally the plan was that we'd go straight to school from here, so we all have our uniforms with us, but I have absolutely no intention of going into school today. In between trying not to cry and trying not to puke, I manage to get myself fully clothed and shove everything of mine into my bag. Then I walk downstairs, hoping that they won't hear me. Maybe they can. Maybe they just don't care. Maybe they're saying, "Typical Nicole, can't face up to anything."

I don't know where to go. I don't want to go home until all my family are gone, so I won't have to face *them*. There's no *way* I'm going to school, and anyway we're not in until eleven anyway. The one person I could have turned to, Mark, is probably still sleeping, and anyway, after last night, I'm going to be avoiding him for a while.

I eventually decide to wait for the bus into town, knowing that by the time I get in there all the shops will be open and I can walk around for a while, or hang around Stephen's Green, or find something to do with myself while I'm wishing that I didn't exist.

Part Three

Aftermath

18

Rachel

Adam's avoiding me.

Of course, I don't realise this at first, I have to be told by Danielle and Caitlin that he is. Then I figure out what feels a little off about today. Not speaking to him. We usually chat a bit at some point during the day, but not today. Of course, I assumed the general sense of weirdness about today was due to other factors. Like at least a quarter of the year being out "sick", or not starting class until eleven, or being exhausted after last night, or the disappointment of not having anything to anticipate and look forward to.

I can't bring myself to care that much about Adam right now. He's fun, sure, and friendly, but apart from that I don't see anything special in him, and I have more important things to think about.

Like the fight with Nicole last night, or Danielle's heartbreak, but even those big important things pale in comparison to what's really on my mind.

As usual, it's my weight. I keep thinking of how much I need to lose. I'm seven and a half stone now, which is good, I guess, because I've lost over a stone, but I still want to lose more. I'm not thin yet, which is weird, because I thought when I got down below eight I'd definitely be skinny. But I'm not yet. I guess seven is what I have to aim for. It's so unfair, though. Danielle weighs eight and a half, and *she's* thin.

I read in one of those magazines that bulimics don't lose as much weight as anorexics, because they still retain some of the food in their stomach. Now, obviously I'm not bulimic – I mean, when they talk about bulimics they don't mean people like me, who just throw up every now and then – but it still could sort of apply to me. If I just stopped eating, instead of eating-and-throwing-up, I might lose more weight, and get thin faster.

And I have to start thinking of calories, as well. Right now I only have a vague idea of the calorie content of every food. You know, like being aware that chocolate is a definite no-no when you're counting calories. There's a table in the Home Ec book I had last year. I wonder is it calories or something useless like fibre content? I'll check when I go home. And if it's not then I'll have a look around the kitchen. I'm sure there'll be something in one of those cookbooks that Mum has and never uses.

Suddenly I'm dying to go home so I can check this out, get this area of my life sorted out, but lunch is over and I've got another three classes to get through.

I'm cheered up mildly when I get an A on some homework we're given back, but then I see that Caitlin got an A as well, so it doesn't really count as much. How can you be the best when other people do as well as you do? It's impossible. If I'd been the only one to get an A I'd be happy. But I wasn't. I was just good. Not exceptional. Just good. Is there anything worse than being average?

Our last class is computers. Blah. It's so boring. We're doing the ECDL, and we're on the word processing module. It's ridiculously easy, but Danielle and Naomi, who are nearest to me, never seem to have a clue what's going on. Naomi's out sick today – she said this morning that she was still hung over and was going home to sleep for the rest of the day – so Danielle's on her own, playing Solitaire. She has Word open, but minimized, so whenever the teacher walks by she just clicks on it and pretends to be actually working.

I decide to take a page out of my sister's book and do the same. I have a blissful half an hour of visiting websites about dieting while being ready to minimize the Internet Explorer window at any time. Then, home.

In a way I'm weirdly resentful of this fight with Nicole. If it hadn't happened, maybe Danielle would be paying more attention to me. Maybe she'd see that I'm doing something I shouldn't be doing. Maybe she can make it all okay. Maybe she can . . . I don't know. I just want her to know. I want to stop feeling so *alone*.

I don't eat all day but it's really hard not to. I tell Mum that I had Spaghetti Hoops earlier so I don't feel like eating dinner, and she accepts it. I tell Danielle that I'm feeling sick after drinking last night and that I can't eat anything. She accepts it.

I stay in my room and try to read, but I keep thinking about food. Food food food. I'd love some chocolate – or crisps – even an *apple* would be nice. But I can't have it. Food equals bad, food equals greedy, food equals fat equals misery.

The words on the page all seem to remind me of food. I slam it shut in frustration and throw it across the room. It falls silently in a pile of clothes, a scream gone unheard

19

Danielle

I ignored Mark all day. I didn't want to talk to him, or even look at him – I was scared I'd start crying, or screaming at him, or generally making a scene. So I avoided him, keeping my head down the whole time, pretending not to notice him walking by as I talked to my friends, even though I was uncomfortably aware of his presence the whole time.

I'm glad Nicole wasn't in school. I'd probably have wrung her neck. I wasn't surprised to find that she'd already left by the time the others woke up. If I were her, I wouldn't have even had the nerve to spend the night.

Okay, I know I'm not perfect. I know I've done my share of shitty things to Nicole. But I never met someone she liked when I knew she liked him. Well, apart from that one time in first year, but we were just kids then, for God's sake! It doesn't count. Besides, she barely knew Kenneth; she just fancied him because he was cute. I *know* Mark. It's completely different.

No one seems to notice the fact that I'm so awkward all day and too scared of humiliating myself to even catch Mark's eye. Either that or they all know what's going on and are trying to be tactful.

Maybe they just assume that I'm obviously over him and think that I'm not bothered by what happened last night. Maybe they don't realise what a sad person I am, to not be able to get over him. I am, I know. I'd *love* to be able to move on, but I can't. I can't force myself to stop liking him and there's a part of me that doesn't want to, that can't imagine a world where I don't fantasise and obsess over Mark.

I feel like screaming. This entire situation is incredibly frustrating and I'm trapped. When I get home it's a mild relief. I don't have to work so hard at being aware of Mark all the time so I can avoid him, but he still haunts me.

"Get out of my head," I mutter at him.

He smirks. He's not leaving.

Oh God, it's happening. I'm finally going crazy. I shake my head to rid myself of the miniature Mark living inside my skull, and go into Rachel's room.

"Haven't you ever heard of knocking?" she snaps as I walk in and plonk myself down on her bed.

"Mark's living inside my head," I tell her.

She bursts out laughing.

"Rache! It's not funny!" I protest, but then I start giggling too. "I'm pathetic, amn't I?"

"Completely," she agrees, grinning.

"I hate Nicole."

"She shouldn't have met him," Rachel agrees.

"You think?"

"It wasn't entirely her fault, though." Rachel is being Reasonable and Mature and Fair again. I respond by rolling my eyes at her.

"Seriously, though . . . Mark obviously wanted to meet her, or he wouldn't have gone along with it. At least, he was so drunk he *thought* he wanted to meet her," she quickly adds. Nice save.

I shrug. Logically I know she's right, but if I start thinking that way then I'll hate Mark for not wanting to meet *me*, and it's a lot easier to hate Nicole.

We're both silent for a couple of minutes, then Rache says in this tiny little voice, "Danielle?"

"Yeah?"

"Do you think I'm fat?"

I'm about to groan and tell her to get a life when I see the look on her face. She's really serious about this.

"No! Rachel, you're not fat. No way. You never have been, and you're not now." I look closely at her, hidden in baggy clothes. "Have you lost weight?"

She nods, but doesn't seem happy about it.

"How much do you weigh now?" I ask.

"Seven and a half stone," she says in that same quiet voice. It's starting to scare me.

"Rachel!" I gasp. We're usually about the same weight, give or take a pound or two, but now she's a whole stone lighter than I am – probably more. And she's only been doing the whole dieting thing for about a month, maybe six weeks at most. But still – I don't think she should have lost that much weight, or that it's healthy for her to weigh that much less than me when we're around the same height and have a similar build, and I'm reasonably slim. And I can't understand why she seems so depressed about weighing seven and a half stone.

"It's not *that* much," she says defensively, tears welling up in her eyes. At first I think she means that a stone isn't that much weight to have lost, but then it hits me. She's talking about her weight.

I'm speechless. I look at her and all I can do is hug her. She's so *thin*. I try to speak, but there's a huge lump in my throat. She's sobbing hard now, shaking. This can't be just because she thinks she weighs too much. It's got to be the whole thing that's been going on lately – the depressing music, the withdrawal, the throwing up. I suddenly don't know if I can handle this, if I know what to do if she tells me what I don't want to hear. I want to know the truth but I'm scared of it as well. I just want her to be my perfect, in-control sister again.

"It's not that much, Rache," is all I can say once I regain my ability to talk without bursting into tears.

She just nods.

I release her and look at her tear-streaked face. "Rache, what's going on?" I ask, my voice getting dangerously trembly again.

"I'm fat. *That's* what's going on," she says softly. She believes every word she's saying.

"You're not. You're skinny – *too* skinny – and it's scaring me."

"I'm not," she says firmly. "Not for lack of trying. God, I've been trying so hard, but it's just not working! I'm still fat!" She starts crying again.

"What do I have to do to convince you you're not?" I demand. "What do you want? What's it going to take to make you stop?"

"I'm not *doing* anything."

"Yeah, I guess that explains why you were puking last night!" I say sarcastically.

"I was sick because I drank too much!" she defends.

"You went off looking for somewhere private to throw up. It took me ages to find you. If you were really sick from drinking you would've used the toilets downstairs! Rache, I know what's going on! I'm not stupid. We all know you want to lose weight. When you find out that someone's getting sick it doesn't take a genius to put two and two together."

Silence.

"Say something," I finally plead.

"Leave me alone," she says quietly.

"Rache . . . come on. You can't keep doing this to yourself."

"Get *out!*" she yells.

"I'll tell Mum," I threaten.

"You wouldn't."

"I'll do it."

"What do I have to do to shut you up?"

"Stop making yourself get sick."

"Done." She looks me straight in the eye. Maybe she means it. I leave.

20

Nicole

I don't feel like going into school on Friday. I'm hung over from going out drinking with people from Mark's road last night, anyway. I don't know them that well, but a couple of them are in my school. It didn't matter. I just wanted to get pissed. That was their aim, too. It worked out well for us all.

Both my parents are usually gone before I leave for school, anyway. When you think about it, it's surprising I manage to go into school at all, with the prospect of skipping it tempting me every morning.

Besides, I prefer avoiding them as much as possible.

I feel like I'm avoiding everyone who used to be a part of my life before Wednesday. (Was that only two days ago? It feels like an eternity.) Avoid the parents because they're mean and don't understand you. Avoid Val because she's too cheery and bouncy. Avoid Luke because he's annoying. Avoid Mark because you met him. Avoid Danielle because you met Mark. Avoid your friends because they hate you.

I end up in town again, wandering around. It's better than being in school, better than being surrounded by people who wish you weren't there, better than facing up to anything.

Whenever I find my thoughts drifting into Niall-land I have to force myself away from there, because I end up feeling sick and disgusted and scared and victimised all at the same time.

Similarly, whenever I think about Mark I feel horrible for meeting him when I wasn't interested.

It seems like it's not safe to think about *anyone* any more, I quickly find out. It's all bad. That's why I keep drinking, to make it go away, to stop having to think about it. Do whatever you can to block it out, that's my new motto, I tell myself as I gulp down the remainder of the vodka in my bag.

21

Rachel

I couldn't stop crying on Thursday night after Danielle left. I curled up into a tiny ball and sobbed for hours. I kept thinking of more things to get upset over, and the tears kept coming.

Hating how fat I was. Hating what I have to do to try to get thin. How awful Danielle's reaction was and the fear in her eyes. Danielle hugging me and making me feeling loved for once, wanting so much to tell her everything but at the same time being reluctant to. Her knowing about it. The power she has now that she does know. The fact that she doesn't really know anything – she understands the actions, but not the motives or the emotions. Me feeling so alone.

I contemplated listening to "All By Myself" and singing along passionately to it, until I realised how sad and Bridget Jones-esque that would be. Although now I'm thinking maybe being like Bridget wouldn't be the worst thing in the world. She ended up getting what she wanted in the end.

I ended up listening to Alanis Morissette's "That I Would Be Good" over and over again. It depressed me. I cried myself to sleep, but I've been doing that a lot lately, I suppose. It's just that at night everything seems much worse.

"I'm *so* glad it's nearly the weekend," Danielle says on our way to school.

Danielle's attitude to school is completely different to mine. She loves the social side of it and hates working. I don't mind the classes – well, most of them – because at least I'm mildly distracted from my usual feeling of not fitting in.

It's like I take up too much space, space that I don't deserve. I sit there but I don't belong there. People around me are laughing and talking and I have nothing of interest to contribute, nothing worthwhile to say. I can't be funny or witty or amusing. So I stay silent, and if someone asks me something I always say something stupid. I'm hopeless.

"Yeah," I say. See? *Hopeless*. Despair washes over me in waves – or maybe they're tsunamis. Either way I'm going to drown. It's only a matter of time.

My feelings towards weekends depend on what I'm doing. If we all go out somewhere, I hate it. We'll go to a disco and it'll be too smoky and too crowded and I'll feel hideous and fat – well, *more* hideous and fat, it's all relative I suppose. If we're all just hanging around talking, that's okay. I can handle it. I don't feel like I'm being judged and compared. If I get to spend the weekend curled up in bed with a book or in front of the TV or listening to CDs, even better. Less pressure, less worrying about what to say or how to dress.

"Heya." Caitlin catches up with us.

"Seven and a bit more hours to go until the weekend!" Danielle informs her.

Caitlin laughs. "Yay! Except I'll be spending my weekend working on projects. It's so depressing. Isn't fourth year meant to be easy?"

"It is," Danielle says. "Just don't bother doing the projects."

That's Danielle-logic for you. And it's then that I remember something.

"Oh, crap," I say.

"What?" Caitlin asks.

"I'm meant to be doing a project on Italy with Nicole."

"It's not due for ages. We'll be friends with her by then," Caitlin reassures.

"What?" Danielle sounds utterly shocked.

"Well, it's not like we're never going to speak to her ever again," Caitlin says reasonably.

"I'm not," Danielle mutters.

"Oh, come on. I hate fighting with people." Caitlin still regrets fighting with Grace. She's that sort of person – even though Grace was the one who met her boyfriend, Caitlin thinks she should have "handled it better" and then maybe they'd still be friends. She's too nice.

"Nicole doesn't count as a person," Danielle snaps.

"Give her a break. We can all be a little bitchy sometimes."

"A *little* bitchy? Did you *hear* her?"

"You've said worse."

"Caitlin, whose side are you *on*, anyway?"

"This isn't about *sides* . . ."

"You're right. It's not. It's about me being right, and her being wrong."

"Oh, for God's sake, Danielle, grow up!" Caitlin snaps, and storms off. We can see her striding off ahead of us, power-walking her way to school.

"I can't believe she's defending Nicole," Danielle says in disgust.

I swallow my "Nicole's not that bad" line and go for a non-committal "Mmmm".

Danielle rants and raves on the way to school while I start to plan the day ahead. I skipped breakfast already, but that's a given at this stage. No lunch – it's going straight in the bin as soon as possible. No going to get crisps or chocolate at lunchtime, either, which is why I've purposely stopped bringing money to school.

I have a craving for a Moro, though. Not so much the biscuit bits in the centre, but the thick chocolate coating and the chewy caramel. Caramel in a Moro bar always seems much chewier than the caramel in a Caramel bar, I don't know why. Plus I like the way you can crunch Moros. Can't do that with Caramels – you can nibble, or you can suck, but you can't crunch.

Or maybe a Time Out. Or a Mars bar. Or a Crunchie. Or maybe all of them.

Bad. Bad Rachel. I know I can't let myself give into the temptation. But I want to, so badly . . .

What was it Oscar Wilde said? "I can resist everything except temptation." Well, that's summing up my personality right about now.

I know I'm going to give in. And I know I'm going to have to take my usual steps to counteract my lack of self control. And I know that'll mean breaking my promise to Danielle – but I think we all know I had no intention of keeping it in the first place.

22

Danielle

So Caitlin's siding with Nicole. Great. Just great.

I reach school in a pretty bad mood. I just want the day to be *over*.

"Hey," Eric greets Rachel and myself when we arrive.

"Hi," I snap.

"Hi, Eric," Rachel smiles and manages to come across as the saner of the Connolly sisters. How unusual.

"So . . ." he says.

"What is it?" I ask impatiently.

"Do you think Caitlin still likes me?"

I roll my eyes. "Who knows, Eric? All I know is she's not the most mentally *stable* person at the moment."

Eric looks confused, and Saint Rachel takes it upon herself to explain. "They had a bit of a fight on the way to school. Listen, I don't know if Caitlin still likes you or not, but I'll talk to her, okay?"

He grins. "Thanks, Rache."

"No problem," she shrugs.

God. She's so . . . I don't know. She seems to be able to deal with everything so well. On one hand she's this super organiser student who can juggle brilliant grades with always being there for her friends – and on the other hand she's that fragile creature I got to see yesterday. I feel like I must have imagined it, seeing her now, so in control. Then I look closer and see that her school uniform is definitely looser than it should be on her. I know she's lost weight, but maybe she still does have everything under control. Maybe she can handle the dieting and throwing up the way she handles life in general. She can't really be doing anything dangerous, can she? I mean . . . it's Rachel.

"What am I doing here?" Naomi groans as she sits down next to me. "My mum would've let me stay at home . . . but, like the idiot I am, I said I'd come in."

I grin. "Yeah, you should've stayed at home – then we wouldn't have had to put up with you."

"You're so sweet, Danielle. It's good to know I'm appreciated. Anyway, has Nicole been in yet?"

"No, and I hope she stays out."

"I was talking to Tony this morning, you know, on Mark's road? He said Nicole went out drinking with them last night, and that she was already pissed by the time she met up with them. She must be pretty miserable if she's drinking that much – I mean, you know the way she usually is." She imitates Nicole, "Of *course* you don't need alcohol to enjoy yourselves."

I smirk. "She's such a hypocrite."

"Still, the poor thing."

"What? Why is everyone feeling so sorry for her? She's a bitch! As you declared passionately about a million times on Wednesday night, remember, Naomi?"

"Yeah, but she seems like she's having a tough time. Come on, don't you remember what she said about her mum calling her a bitch all the time? And you were the one to start the fight."

Was I? I replay that night in my mind. Hmm. I seem to have been conveniently forgetting about that itsy-bitsy fact, but still – it wasn't like I didn't have a reason.

"She slagged you off," I try gaining Naomi's sympathy once more.

"No, she didn't," Naomi says firmly.

"You know what I *mean*."

"It wasn't like she said anything that wasn't true, Danielle, so can we drop this? Please?"

"Fine! But I still don't think she deserves anyone's sympathy."

Naomi nods. "Okay. Whatever." She's huffy.

"Aw, come on. Don't be like that," I plead. "I'm fighting with enough people already."

"So one more won't make a difference, then," she says, but grinning now.

I smile. "You're the worst person to fight with. You're so evil."

She beams. "Thanks."

French this year is spent alternating between watching

videos (French ones, unfortunately) and improving our communication skills (using the French language, again unfortunately).

I personally spend French classes doodling on anything available, and talking to my friends.

As you can see, the teachers sometimes overestimate how much work we're willing to put into their class.

Today I'm talking to Naomi about Mark, but I'm not as angry as I was – all the Mark-related emotions seem to be fading in intensity. It's weird. I'm saying the words that I should be saying, but they seem so hollow. It's not me at all. It's what I used to be. I mean, when I think of Nicole and Mark together it upsets me a little, but that's it.

It's probably nothing, I tell myself. Tomorrow I'll be back to being obsessed with him, and everything can go back to normal.

I'm interrupted by the French teacher, who declares dramatically that we are not *parlezing en français*. I hate French teachers that speak French. It's scary, and unproductive. I mean, if we *understood* French, we wouldn't need to be doing it in school, would we?

And these are the people responsible for our education. It really makes you wonder.

23

Nicole

My mother likes to pretend she doesn't need sleeping pills, because she acts like pills are a sign of weakness. She thinks she gives off the impression of a strong, capable woman, instead of one dependent on cigarettes and sleeping pills.

It was the pills that gave me the idea. I was thinking about them when I was in town, sort of vaguely wandering through the avenues of my mind.

I mean, I just want it to be over, right?

I want to forget. I want to make it all go away.

I can't do it tonight; she'll notice if I take them now when she goes for them later. And that's not what I want to happen. She might get mad, and if it doesn't work then I have to face the consequences, and it's just too much to handle right now.

But tomorrow morning . . . yeah, tomorrow. That's the day.

24

Rachel

Why did I tell Eric I'd talk to Caitlin? Why? I hate having to be the go-between, the messenger. Plus, I still get nervous around Eric. Not because I still fancy him, just because I don't know him that well any more, and I'm always worrying about whether I'm acting like I still fancy him, and it's a huge horrible circle of anxiety and wondering.

Did I always worry this much, or is it a recent thing? It feels like it's always been this way, me panicking over every little thing.

I hate it.

I start to wonder if it's always going to be this way, and then I remember. All I have to do is get thin, and everything else falls into place. Once I'm really skinny I won't get nervous around Eric, because I'll look great, and I'll feel great.

It's that simple. Right? Oh, I know it might sound a little

crazy, but I just *know* I'd be more confident if I was thin. I wouldn't be constantly worrying about the other person looking at me and thinking how incredibly fat I was. Everything would be much easier. I can't wait.

I walk home with Caitlin and deduce that no, she is not interested in Eric any more. How do I come to this conclusion? Elementary, my dear Watson.

"I'm not interested in Eric any more," she says firmly.

Right so. That's my job done, then.

We wind up discussing the whole Fight Saga.

"I'm not taking Nicole's side," Caitlin says, "but I'm not taking Danielle's, either. I mean, I feel like I'm the only one who realises she played a pretty big part in all this, you know?"

"Yeah, I know what you mean."

"I know Nicole shouldn't have acted that way, but we all make mistakes! And Danielle acting like *she's* so perfect . . . that just annoyed me."

"She's really upset about Mark, though," I volunteer, feeling like I should be sticking up for my sister.

Caitlin sighs. "I know she is. But how long are we meant to put up with hearing her go on and on about Mark? They're not even together any more! I'm getting sick of it."

"Okay, so Danielle can be a *little* self-involved . . ."

"A *little?*" Caitlin demands.

I'm getting fed up of talking to her. She's being bitchy, and not at all like the kind, thoughtful person I thought she was. I hate how much everyone's changed in the last couple of days. It feels like I'm living in a parallel universe where everyone looks the same (skinny, beautiful, perfect) but their personalities are completely different. No one seems to have changed for the better. I'm relieved to get home.

I'm absolutely starving. For an entire hour I manage to go without food, feeling sort of proud but not really. It's not that big an achievement. I should be able to go for longer. I haven't eaten all day. I should be able to keep that up – but I succumb.

I have to get rid of it, but it seems like I have absolutely no privacy. When I go into the bathroom Mum and Dad are talking on the landing, and I don't dare risk it, even with the taps turned on. Then Dad walks downstairs and I think I'll be safe, until I realise Mum's still there, at the door to Danielle's room, talking to her about school or something.

Why can't they just all leave and give me some *space?* I feel like I'm trapped. All you need are bars on the window and you'd recognise the house for what it really is.

I wake up late on Saturday morning as a result of a night spent tossing and turning. Dad's the only one still around. He informs me that Mum's gone shopping with a couple of her friends (the thought of forty-year-old women shopping in groups just seems *wrong*) and that Danielle's gone to someone's house.

"Whose house?" I enquire.

But of course, he doesn't know. All of our friends merge

into one in his mind. Mum, on the other hand, knows the names of everyone – purely so she can complain about each one individually. "That Naomi's too innocent-looking. I don't trust her" or "Nicole's a bad influence". She likes Caitlin because she's a good student, and Michelle because she goes to a Gaelscoil and therefore must be a wonderful person. I don't quite follow her reasoning on that one. If I didn't know Michelle I'd be of the mind that anyone who would willing attend an all-Irish school for five years needed a straitjacket.

"Did she bring her mobile?" I ask Dad.

He shrugs. "Rachel, how am I supposed to know? I presume she has it with her. What's the point in us buying the two of you phones if you never use them?"

"So that we can put pretty covers on them," I kid. To him, the thought of phone-as-fashion-accessory is absolutely unthinkable. *He* has this hideous chunky thing that's about five years old and looks more like a walkie-talkie than a mobile, but it "does the job".

He rolls his eyes, and I have breakfast – well, coffee. No milk, no sugar. I used to hate the taste but I'm getting used to it, since it wakes me up in the mornings and I need *some* way of finding the energy to get through the day.

At around two the doorbell rings. Dad calls to me to get it. Reluctantly, I do so. I've started avoiding answering the door so I don't have to deal with people – it just seems easier.

It's Mark. Shit. I know I look terrible, and I wish I didn't. It's not that I fancy him any more – we'll leave that up to my wacky sister – but I just hate people seeing me when I'm not at my best, when I haven't had a chance to prepare and make myself look less awful than I usually do. Some people like to accentuate their positive features, but all I want to do is try to camouflage the negative ones. Maybe if I *had* positive features I'd be different.

"Heya, Rache. Is Danielle in?"

"Nah, she's gone out," I say.

"Oh, right. You don't know where?"

I shrug. "No idea. She left before I got up."

"Oh," he sighs.

"What's up?" I enquire.

He shrugs. "Just wanted to talk to her, but I'll come around later."

"I'll tell her you called – this wouldn't be about Nicole, would it?"

He smiles sheepishly. "Yeah, sort of. I just wanted to see if she's okay with it – she's been avoiding me, you know?"

"I noticed, yeah," I grin.

"She's not okay with it, is she?" he says. Oh, *so* perceptive.

"Not exactly," I reply.

He half-grins, half-frowns. "Great."

Dad comes out into the hall. "Oh, hello, Mark. Are you going to come in?"

"Hiya," Mark nods. "Nah, it's fine. I'll be leaving in a sec, anyway."

"What are you going to say to Danielle later?" I say quietly.

"No idea. What do you think?" he replies.

25

Danielle

"No, Michelle, I'm not giving you one. It's a disgusting habit," Naomi lectures Michelle.

"Is that so?" Michelle asks, raising an eyebrow.

I have to admit that Naomi might be more convincing if she wasn't on her fifth cigarette today. Then again, she believes what she's saying. She knows it's disgusting, but she loves it anyway.

On Wednesday night I gave in and had a cigarette for the first time in years; now on Saturday I'm doing it again. Okay, so I have no willpower. So what?

"Yes," Naomi says firmly. "I'm not going to let you ruin your health."

"You're letting me," I point out.

"Yeah, but you don't count," she kids.

I stick my tongue out at her.

"Come on. Just give me one," Michelle pleads.

Naomi finally gives in. Michelle smirks triumphantly and lights up.

We're in Naomi's house, half-watching MTV. It's still too early – about half two in the afternoon – for us to make much conversation. Michelle is here to avoid her mother, who she's fighting with (her "good child" persona gone out the window), and I'm here because of boredom. I woke up early but couldn't get back to sleep, and after sitting around watching cartoons for hours, I decided I needed to get out of the house or else I'd go crazy.

Besides, the Rachel thing is getting to me.

How can she be doing something so *stupid?* And how could this have been going on without me noticing? No, I noticed something was up, but I didn't want to believe it because I like to think Rache has got everything figured out. I was scared to ask in case of – well, I don't know, in case I was overreacting. In case she'd laugh at me.

God, it seems so stupid now. I was worried about embarrassing myself by asking, and it turns out she's doing something that's classified as a *disorder*. The word in itself is scary when it's being applied to someone so close to you. And Rache and I *are* close. Sure, we fight loads, and she just doesn't understand me half the time and I get jealous of her sometimes, but she's still my sister, my friend, and I hate the situation as it is now.

In a way I'm pissed off with her for all this. Like, I don't know, she's doing it for attention or something, or . . . I resent her for making me worry, or *something*. And then I feel guilty because I'm meant to be concerned and trying to help and not supposed to hate her at all for any of this.

Then sometimes I go into denial mode. It's not that bad. Rachel doesn't have a problem. Everything's going to be fine.

It keeps on going round and round in my head like a hamster running around on one of those wheels, you know? The poor little creature keeps going, but never really gets anywhere.

Anyway, that's why I feel like I need to talk to my friends.

But now I'm wondering if I should. I mean, they have their own issues to deal with, their own problems. It's not fair for me to dump everything on them, even if it might make me feel better. It'd be completely selfish.

Oh, who cares, I'm going to be selfish. So what if it makes me a bad person? Nobody's perfect. I'm going to tell them.

"Guys?" I say cautiously. "Have you noticed anything, um, weird about Rache lately?"

Michelle turns to me. "Yeah."

Naomi nods. "She's been really quiet – it's like she's scared of saying anything. Except on Junior Cert night, with Nicole. She was so confident then. I don't know, it's like she's got all this stuff to say but she's holding back because she's terrified of speaking up."

"Like we're going to judge her or something," Michelle adds. "I know she's insecure and all, but it's been really bad lately."

Rachel, insecure? I still have trouble linking those two concepts. Yeah, I know she worries about what people think of her a lot, but everyone likes her, so I assume that because it's a moot point, she doesn't have to worry any more, even though she does. It's just hard to listen to someone so perfect go on about how no one really likes them – you automatically assume they're fishing for compliments.

"Not to mention the weight thing," Naomi says. "Have you talked to her about that? She seems . . . totally preoccupied."

"I noticed," I mutter.

"Like sometimes in school," Naomi continues, "she'll just be staring at her stomach in, like, *horror*, and then start pulling on her jumper and crossing her arms and stuff, like she doesn't want anyone to see what she looks like. But she's so skinny!"

I didn't even notice that. The staring thing, I mean. Either I'm completely oblivious, or Naomi's been paying an unusual amount of attention to Rache. I decide I don't want to know.

Michelle looks shocked. "I didn't know it was that bad – that sounds really serious."

"It gets worse," I tell her. "She's been making herself get sick."

"*What?*" Michelle seems to be on the verge of collapsing any moment now. "God, no! Are you sure?"

"Of course I'm sure!" I say.

"We have to talk to her," Naomi says quietly.

"I tried – she got really upset, but she said she'd stop," I inform them.

"So that's good, right? She's going to stop doing it," Michelle's relieved.

"She lied. I heard her last night."

"Oh."

"Did you say anything to her?" Naomi enquires. "Last night, I mean."

I shrug. "No. She thinks I don't know."

"Maybe she just slipped up and she's not going to do it any more," Michelle suggests hopefully.

"Yeah. Right," Naomi rolls her eyes.

"She's been doing it for weeks now – I don't think she *can* stop," I say.

"You should tell your mum," Michelle says.

"No way," I insist. That's just out of the question. I know she's an adult, but getting an adult involved in something like this isn't always the answer. Besides, Michelle doesn't seem to understand the severe lack of non-school-related communication that Rache and I have with our mum. Michelle thinks our mum's really nice – but I think her mum's really nice, and Michelle can't stand her half the time. No one ever seems to get along with their own parents.

"Your dad?" she suggests.

I don't have much faith in my dad's situation-handling abilities, either. She can tell from the look on my face.

"Come on, you have to tell *someone*."

"Why?" I demand. "I told you guys, isn't that enough?

What makes you think either of my parents is going to be able to wave a magic wand and make everything better? That's not going to happen. They can't do anything that we can't do."

"Okay, so what *are* we going to do?" Naomi demands.

"I don't *know*," I snap. Why isn't this working out the way I thought it would? I expected that telling my friends would make everything better, but they don't have magic wands either. They can't solve this. "Look, forget I ever said anything," I say, getting up and leaving the room.

"Danielle!" Naomi calls after me.

I slam the door and storm out. When I get to my house I see Caitlin, Mark and Rachel at the front door, looking serious. Oh God. Something's happened. Caitlin is crying, and it doesn't look like the-guy-I-like-doesn't-like-me tears, either.

"What happened?" I ask, noting the way Mark has his arm protectively around Rachel with an ache.

"Caitlin just came over to tell us," Mark explains, looking pale. "Nicole's been rushed off to hospital."

I panic. "Why? What – what's wrong with her?" Please let her be okay, please, please. I don't care if Mark is madly in love with her. Just please let her be okay!

No one wants to say anything. Then Rache speaks, the one word that sends me running upstairs and pulling the bedcovers over my head in a pathetic attempt to make it all go away.

"Overdose."

26

Nicole

The first person I see when I wake up is Val. "Hey, babe," she grins.

"Val?" I frown. What's she doing in my room? And then I look around. This isn't my room.

"Where am I?" I ask, and then roll my eyes. Stupid question. I'm in the hospital; I can figure out that much. It looks like a hospital room. It *feels* like one. What I don't get is *why*.

"Hospital," she smiles, knowing that I know the answer already. "You don't remember what happened?"

I shake my head. Everything's sort of hazy, especially the last couple of days. I have a vague feeling that alcohol was involved in that haze, and then . . .

Yeah. I remember. I remember counting out the pills. I remember wanting to die. But I didn't. Did I? It seems silly now even thinking about that, like it's some other girl, some crazy alternative-universe Nicole who took the pills.

"You took a bunch of your mam's sleeping pills," Val relates softly. "Everyone had gone out, but I came back to get my keys, and I found you in your room with the bottle beside you. Anyway, being me, I spent a couple of minutes freaking out and bawling my eyes out before being sensible and calling an ambulance. Your mam and dad are on their way here, by the way."

"Are they pissed off?" I picture my parents arriving to yell at me for causing all this hassle.

Val looks at me in surprise. "God, no! They're worried, sure, but that's it."

Silence.

"I guess you saved my life, huh?" I say shakily.

She gives me a hug. "The doctors told me you hadn't taken enough to kill yourself," she says. "But they said it looked like you were trying to."

I shrug.

"Were you?" she presses.

"I – I don't know. I thought I was."

"Why?" she finally bursts out, tears running down her face. I'm crying too.

Why. That's a good question. I don't have an answer for her. Were my problems really so big that I thought the only way to escape was by dying? Things couldn't have been that bad, could they? Things are *never* so bad that there's no way out.

Mum and Dad arrive in later. Big emotional scene. I just want to go home, but I have to stay in hospital for a while longer so that they can make sure there's no permanent damage. Plus they want me to see a shrink. Whoop dee doo. Another option suggested is family counselling, but I have a serious problem with the "family" part of that. I think the Robinson clan can all do without baring our souls to one another.

Maybe that's part of the problem. None of us really want to talk to each other. Yelling is okay, or trivial chatter, but when it comes down to anything remotely serious we all run away screaming in terror.

But hey, my family isn't my problem. Once I finish school I'm going to be out of here. All I have to do is try to survive the next couple of years.

I keep thinking about what everyone at school's going to say. Val told me that Caitlin already knows. I wonder if she, or anyone else, will even care. I wonder what Mark's going to think. I wonder how the teachers will react. I wonder if Mrs Connolly will take this to mean that I'm definitely an unsuitable friend for her precious daughters.

I don't really like imagining what it's going to be like, but I know I'll have to face up to it soon. It sucks. It's going to be hard.

But it beats dying, any day.

27

Rachel

It's like that Pringles ad – once you pop, you can't stop? Once I start crying I find it hard to stop. My life has turned into a tear factory.

All the way to the hospital I'm praying that Nicole's okay.

Danielle's at home, in bed. She won't get up – she's been there ever since she heard about Nicole. It was only a couple of hours ago. Feels like a century. She just lies there, curled into a ball. I tried talking to her but she just turns over and ignores me.

Mum is driving me to the hospital. To my great surprise, she expresses concern for Nicole. And here I thought she'd be – well, I'm not sure, but I was expecting a lot more negativity from her.

She offered to give Caitlin or Mark a lift, but they refused. I think they're scared, or something. Maybe they just don't want to see her in hospital. I'm not crazy about hospitals myself, but it doesn't seem to matter any more when I think of Nicole in there.

It seems to be putting a lot of things in perspective. It's like, for the last month or so, all I've really been able to think about is the way I look, how much I weigh, what other people think of me. My whole world revolved around that, and suddenly it's expanded and there's a lot more going on, including one of my best friends being in hospital right now, maybe dead. No. Don't think that. She's going to be fine.

I remember the first time I really hung out with Nicole. It was in second year. She'd been suspended and I went with Danielle and a couple of others over to her house during their lunchtime. After they went back to school, I stayed, and I was really flattered that she wanted me to stay. She was, to me, the coolest person ever, and I desperately wanted her to like me. We got on really well, and one day a few months later I told her about really wanting her to think I was cool, too. She laughed and said she'd been like that, too.

And that made me feel great, because someone actually thought I was cool, someone as confident and sophisticated as Nicole.

I suddenly realise that she doesn't think of me as the fat boring girl. Of course she doesn't. She's sweet, but if she doesn't like someone, they find out about it pretty quickly. She doesn't go around thinking "Rachel would be so much more interesting if she lost weight".

Neither does Danielle, or Michelle, or Naomi, or Caitlin. I think about what I said to Danielle on Thursday morning about Naomi. *"We're her friends. It's not like we're going to turn against her or anything."* I knew that we weren't going to suddenly exclude someone because they were different. I knew that, despite how superficial we can seem, we were friends.

Why did I think that everyone was constantly judging and criticising me? They weren't. They're my *friends*.

We don't lie to each other, either. I should have believed them when they told me I was skinny. No one tells a fat girl that she's skinny – they either find a word like "fine" or "great" to use, or else change the subject completely. When people tell you you're skinny, they're not doing it to provoke the little voice inside your head into screaming "They're lying!". They're telling you the truth.

I'm not fat. I know that now. I also know that it doesn't matter how a person looks, not really. Is there any point in being thin if your entire world is centred around that thinness? I mean, I wanted to be thin so that people would like me. Like I was a total social outcast.

I've felt like an outsider plenty of times, but looking back, I've never actually *been* one. I've never been amazingly popular but I've always had friends. Michelle, ever since primary school. Caitlin, for nearly as long. Nicole, who's always tried to make me feel a part of things. Danielle, who despite her faults isn't the worst sister in the world. (Close at times, but not quite.)

Thinking about Nicole now, I feel like a self-indulgent bitch, letting my minor insecurities take over my life.

God, I hope she's okay.

28

Danielle

Right now I know exactly how Nicole felt when she put those pills into her mouth. Like everything that could go wrong has gone wrong, and you don't see any point in continuing to live. In fact, you feel like it's going to take too much energy to go on – so you want to stop it.

I'm trying to sleep, but it won't come – unsurprisingly, as it's a Saturday afternoon. I want it all to go away.

Everything. Rachel being bulimic – that word feels overly scientific for the grossness of what she's doing – and Nicole maybe dead and Mark kissing Nicole and then having his arm around Rachel and I don't care if it was purely to comfort her, I'm still jealous and I hate Rachel for being so pretty and perfect and not being happy with it and I hate her for going to the hospital to see Nicole. I hate Nicole for being gorgeous and for getting Mark to like her and for doing something so stupid. I'm mad because I think on the one hand she's doing this for attention or to make us feel guilty for fighting with her, and I'm mad because it's working a little bit. But I'm still angry with her for what she did, and her pulling a stunt like this isn't going to change that. Then I feel bad for thinking that way, because Rachel doesn't. She's ready to forgive and forget in these circumstances. Which makes me think that I'm a terrible person, and then I hate Rachel even more for being so *good*.

It just keeps going.

I hate Mark for liking everyone else more than me. I hate Naomi because I'm pretty sure she has a crush on Rachel, and that's going to be awkward, and I'm annoyed that she's making things awkward. God, I know she can't help it, I know I'm being a horrible bigoted bitch for just wanting her to be *normal*, but I can't stop myself from thinking it. I hate Caitlin for siding with Nicole and for being the one who told us what had happened to her.

Why won't it stop?

I don't want to ever get out of bed. I just want to close my eyes. I want it to *stop*.

29

Nicole

"I feel like all I've been doing lately is cry," Rachel tells me with a laugh.

"Tell me about it," I nod.

"I'm glad you're okay," she says.

"Me too," I grin. "How are you doing?"

"Me?" She looks surprised.

"Yeah, *you*, Rache. How's everything going for you?"

She smiles. "It's okay."

"Really?"

"No. But I'm working on it."

"You want to talk about it?"

"Yeah, but not now, not when you're still here."

I shrug. "I'm fine. Come on, tell me."

"You sure you want to hear this now?" Rachel asks, and I know it's serious.

"God, what have you done, murdered someone?" I joke.

She smiles. "Not quite."

We're both silent for a while and then she says, "I've been totally obsessed with my weight lately."

"Yeah, I noticed," I say softly.

"I don't know why, really. I guess I thought that if I got skinny suddenly my life would become wonderful."

"It doesn't work that way, though, does it?"

"Nope. I wanted to think it did, though. So, I did some pretty stupid stuff. Stopped eating, for one thing. Except I ended up stuffing my face with chocolate half the time, because I was so hungry – and then I'd feel like a complete pig. So I had to get rid of it."

I stare at her in horror. She makes a fingers-down-the-throat gesture. Maybe I didn't want to hear this.

She just shrugs. "Like I said, pretty stupid, huh?"

All I can do is nod. When I've regained the power of speech I ask, "Why didn't you tell me?"

"I just did," she laughs.

"You know what I mean." In spite of myself, and the seriousness of it all, I grin.

"Like, hey Nicole, how's it going? By the way I'm making myself throw up after everything I eat?" she raises an eyebrow. "I don't know. There was just never a good time, and I didn't think anyone really cared about me, anyway."

"Nutcase. We all love you."

"Awwww," she smiles.

"We should hug. Just to make this even cheesier," I suggest.

134

She rolls her eyes, but hugs me anyway.

"You want to hear about Niall?" I ask her sometime later.

She nods.

So I start talking, knowing I can trust her, especially after what she's shared with me. "He was this guy I liked last summer. Total ride. I was obsessed with him. I flirted with him and got my hopes up, until I saw him with another girl."

Rachel makes a sympathetic face.

"Of course, I was so crazy about him that I kept making excuses. I told myself he didn't really like her, he liked me . . . and eventually went over to his house to try and uh, seduce him."

Rache raises an eyebrow and then smiles. "Do I want the details?"

"No, definitely not. Let's just say I made a fool of myself and was completely embarrassed and hurt, but still couldn't get over him. Anyway, I spent the rest of the summer licking my wounds. Then I ran into him on Junior Cert night."

"What happened?"

"He decided he wanted to sleep with me after all," I say. "Only I didn't want to any more. I went inside, terrified out of my mind, and found Mark. And you can imagine what happened next."

"Yeah, I think I can."

"I feel shitty for using him like that. He's been a really good friend to me about the whole Niall thing, and now I'm avoiding him."

"Mark knew about Niall?" she asks, looking hurt.

"Yeah." I sigh. "Look, Rache, it wasn't that I didn't *want* to tell you. It was just – okay, I didn't want to tell you, but it was only because I thought you'd look down on me or something. I wasn't exactly proud of it, and I didn't want you thinking I was really pathetic. Besides, I wasn't so sure that anyone cared about me, either."

"We're some pair, aren't we?" she asks. "Feeling sorry for ourselves because no one loves us . . ."

I smile. "I know. We're hopeless. But things don't seem as bad as they used to be."

"Really?"

"Yeah. And I'm glad we're talking again."

"Yeah, it was a long two days. I don't know how I coped."

"Oh, shut up!"

"You know I missed you really," she laughs.

Yeah. I missed her too. It's good to have a friend to talk to again.

30

Rachel

I'm still smiling when I leave the hospital – I can't remember the last time I laughed so much. Even though me and Nicole went over some pretty serious stuff, we both ended up happier than either of us were before we talked. Which sounds really corny, I know.

"How was she?" Mum asks as we get into the car.

"Better than I thought she'd be," I tell her.

"I was talking to her mother while you were in there. Apparently she's going to be seeing a therapist for the next couple of months."

"She mentioned that, yeah. She doesn't sound too thrilled about it."

"Probably not, but it'll be good for her, help her sort things out. She must have been very troubled to try and take her own life like that."

(Yeah. Troubled. Just like, say, someone who makes

herself throw up after eating because she's terrified of getting fat?)

"Mmmm," I agree.

(Mum, why don't you see it? How come you can go on about some "poor girl" and her problems when you don't see what's right under your nose?)

But I've already decided I'm going to stop, I remind myself. Today's the first day of the rest of my life. (There I go again with the corniness.) From now on, no more throwing up. It's gross. It's disgusting.

And you are not fat, I tell myself.

On Saturday evening Caitlin calls around and I join her and a couple of others from school out on the green. Usually I'd make an excuse, but the new and improved Rachel Connolly doesn't.

"How's Nicole doing?" Adam asks.

Word has gotten out that she's okay. Amazing how quickly news spreads – by the time I got back from the hospital the entire estate knew that Nicole Robinson had taken an overdose (although there was one group who were under the impression she'd tried to slit her wrists) and an hour later they all knew she was going to be fine.

"She's all right," I say. "We talked for ages. She's in a pretty good mood, all things considered."

"God. I don't know how she could have done it," Tara says.

"I can, sort of," Donal speaks up, and heads swivel in his direction. He goes red at the sudden attention. "I'm just saying. I mean, I don't think I'd actually ever *do* it – but it's not like I haven't thought about it."

"Yeah, I know what you mean," Liz nods.

I suddenly understand what people mean when they talk about depressed teenagers. Is everyone I know like this? I've never thought about killing myself.

Like you can talk, Rache, I remind myself. But still – taking pills or hanging yourself or whatever is a lot more serious than what I've been doing, and it scares me that the people I hang out with have considered doing it, and that one of my best friends actually has.

It suddenly hits me – this is it. Growing up. Or maybe it's not. Maybe it's just stupid teenage angst, and the growing up part comes next. I don't know. I'm not an adult yet; I'm barely a teenager, and I'm not sure if I'm ready to handle anything remotely grown-up like.

No one's drinking tonight, which is unusual. I think it's a result of the Nicole-trauma. We're suddenly very wary of what we put into our bodies. It's not unusual for me, but it's weird to see everyone doing it. Still, I'd bet my life savings – saying it that way sounds better than saying "the two hundred pounds in my bank account", more dramatic – that by next week they're all going to be drinking again.

Another effect of the trauma, for lack of a better word and because "the suicide attempt of our friend" sounds too awful, is that barriers are broken down. Caitlin and I haven't really spoken to Tara or Liz outside of school for ages, yet here we are now, all hanging out together. Adam doesn't seem to mind me being here. I wonder if he's still annoyed with me for not meeting him on Junior Cert night. It must've been embarrassing for him to be rejected, even if it was only by me.

He's really cute, you know. I mean, step outside the tiny world that is Rachel's weight-related-obsession and you find yourself really seeing some people for the first time.

I'm not saying I want to go out with him, but appreciating him from afar – or near, even – couldn't hurt. It's kind of fun to feel the beginnings of a crush again – it's a welcome distraction from everything else that's going on.

"I don't, personally," Adam says. "I just don't get how anyone could *want* to . . ." he trails off, not wanting to say the words.

Caitlin nods. "Yeah. I don't, either."

"Why do you think she did it?" Tara asks quietly. "I mean, Nicole's not exactly miserable, you know. She's really pretty, for one thing, and she always seems so happy."

"*Seems* happy. Obviously she wasn't," Donal points out.

"Rache, did she tell you anything?" Adam asks. "I mean, not that I'm asking you to tell us something personal . . . just, you know, in general . . . if that's okay with you . . . I mean . . ."

He's babbling, and blushing.

I grin, as does everyone else. "You know, you're cute when you blush," I tell him.

Oh my God! Did I, little mousy me, just say that?

(Confident, Rachel. Be confident.)

Now he's blushing even more, but looking slightly pleased.

To bring everyone's attention back to the matter at hand, and stop them from winking and smirking knowingly, I say, "Nicole didn't really say what it was – I don't think she really knows why, just that she was really miserable at the time and thought it was the only way out. She said it's like it was someone else who did it, now."

"Poor her," Adam says sympathetically, looking right at me.

Tara and Donal burst out laughing. So much for getting back to the real issue.

"It's not funny!" Adam exclaims, blushing again.

I wasn't lying. He *is* cute when he blushes. Well, *cuter*.

"He's right. It isn't," Caitlin says. "Come on, guys, you look like you're having a fit or something."

Tara and Donal try to act calm and non-hysterical. It works for about ten seconds. Then they start again.

I roll my eyes. "Nutcases," I say.

"Let's ignore them," Adam suggests.

"I like that idea."

"It's good, isn't it?"

"Up there with the invention of the wheel."

He grins. I practically melt. Yep, it's serious crush territory, all right.

31

Danielle

"I'm not going to school, Mum," I tell her firmly on Monday morning, turning over in bed.

She doesn't seem to understand that this is the point where she's meant to leave my bedroom so I can go back to hiding from civilisation. She hovers there.

"Nicole's fine, you know," she says. "In fact, she might even go into school today, seeing as she's out of hospital."

"I know," I say dully. She doesn't get it. Nicole surviving doesn't make it all better, doesn't mean that everything's suddenly okay. She doesn't get that there must have been a reason for Nicole trying to kill herself and that the reason probably hasn't vanished into thin air since Saturday. It's still there. She could do it again, maybe succeed this time. I don't want that to happen, but I don't want to face her, either.

"There's no point in you staying in bed all day," she continues. "It's not like you're going to make everything stop happening just by hiding from it."

No, but at least I won't have to be there when it happens and have to deal with it.

"Just go, Mum," I say.

"You're not getting out of bed?" she checks one last time.

"No."

"Fine. But you're going into school tomorrow, is that clear?"

"No."

"Danielle, I'm being very fair about this. I'm not going to make you go in today, but I'm not going to let you lie in bed all day tomorrow as well."

"Fine." Maybe now she'll leave. There's no chance of me going into school tomorrow either, but I'll say anything to get her to just leave me alone.

In the darkness that thought comes again. Was it my fault that Nicole –

No, no, no! It's the worst of the thoughts that are haunting me, the one that tears me up inside.

It wasn't my fault. It wasn't my fault. Think of Nicole and Mark kissing, him running his hands through her blonde hair looking as if he was in heaven, her hands on his back moving gradually downwards, their mouths pressed together so hard that you can't tell where one ends and the other begins.

It hurts. I'm jealous of her and I'm angry with him. A sort of mild anger now, but still angry.

Think of that. Just keep thinking of that and everything's going to be okay.

32

Nicole

"Tell me why I don't like Mondays. Tell me why I don't like Mondays," I sing as I walk down the corridor with Rachel on – surprise – Monday morning.

Mum said I could stay at home today, but I declined. I had a good reason at the time, but now, in school, I'm starting to think I'm crazy for not taking the day off.

What possible reason could I have for actually wanting to come into school, you ask? I wanted everyone to see that I was fine. I figured that I might as well get the whole commotion of returning to school post-suicide-attempt thing out of the way as soon as possible. Plus, in my then-optimistic, live-life-to-the-full mood, I was actually looking forward to being back in school and having my mind opened to new ideas and learning new –

Okay, crazy. But I promise you, that insanity was only temporary. I'm now back to normal, completely resenting the fact that I have to be in school for the next three years.

"Tori Amos covered that on her last album," muses Rachel as she listens to me sing. Another difference between her and Danielle – her sister would be telling me what a crap voice I have. Of course, I have absolutely no idea who Tori Amos is. I nod and smile like I know what she's talking about, though.

"I wanna shoo-ooooooooo-oot . . . the whole day down," I finish.

"Remind me never to let you near a gun," she jokes.

"They wouldn't let me have one," I say mournfully. "Say I'd probably do something stupid. Like shoot a bunch of people. I'd only kill a couple of the teachers . . . it'd be for the good of the school. Maybe even the entire world."

Rachel nods. "Yeah. They might even name a day after you. Nicole Day. And every year there'd be a parade . . ."

"I like this!" I say enthusiastically.

We continue planning the mythical Nicole Day (September 23 every year) and have reached the stage with Ewan McGregor making a speech about me (look, if you're going to fantasise, do it right, for God's sake) when we reach Geography, our first class on a Monday. Mark's not in. Thank God.

"Hey, guys," Caitlin greets us as we sit down. The teacher, Mr Matthews (also answers to the name of Ted, even though his first name is Geoff), arrives in right after us, so there's no time for the class to surround me with questions and false concern. Maybe they wouldn't have anyway. I was probably overreacting – no one's going to pay that much attention to me, really.

"Ted! Ted!" Sean says.

"Sean. What can I do for you?" Mr Matthews asks.

"Can we watch the video?"

"Most emphatically not! Transition Year is not a time for watching *videos*. We are here to work, children, and work we shall."

Sean looks horrified.

Mr Matthews just smirks. "Right, everybody, get into your pairs for the projects. You've got the class to discuss them."

We all grin. He's a pretty sound guy, even if he is a little wacky. He knows full well we're going to spend the entire class chatting about anything *but* our projects. He also knows that we need a non-stressful class first thing on a Monday morning.

"Nicole, hey, where were you last week?" a pseudo-concerned Laura asks.

"Out sick," I reply. With my eyes I dare her to challenge my answer, or to bring It up.

"Better now?" she enquires, looking disappointed.

I nod. "Yep. Thanks for asking." My smile is about as genuine as her sympathy.

The next person to stop by is Brian, who isn't so subtle. "Nicole. What the hell are you doing in school? I thought you topped yourself."

"Brian!" Rachel exclaims in horror.

"Do I look dead to you?" I ask him sweetly.

"Nah, you look gorgeous," he grins.

I resist the urge to shudder until he leaves.

"Ugh! What does Michelle see in him?" I ask.

Rachel shrugs. "No idea."

"Heya," Adam joins us, sitting on Rachel's desk.

"Hey, Adam," I smile, being sincere this time. He's all right. Besides, he seems more interested in Rachel than he is in me. She's not completely oblivious, either, and appears to be even enjoying the attention.

"Hi," Rachel smiles.

He grins back at her.

"Did you miss me?" she asks.

"Yeah. I haven't been able to get you out of my head," he responds.

While they flirt, I feel very much like a third wheel. I turn to Caitlin and she smiles knowingly. "Sickening, huh?"

"Yeah," I agree. "How long have they been like this?"

"Too long."

"Go on."

"Since Saturday night – but that's still too long. I think I might puke."

I think of Rachel. "Please don't."

"I'll try, but I'm not making any promises. How are you, anyway?"

"All right," I answer. At the moment. I still hate the fact that people feel like they have the right to ask about my personal life just because of what happened, and I know that it's only beginning with Laura and Brian, but I can't exactly tell that to Caitlin, can I? The act has been committed, it's over, I'm out of hospital, everything's meant to be okay now. I have to be happy and upbeat and perky.

I shudder at the thought. That description makes me sound like Sabrina. Before you know it I'll be pointing my finger at everything and my big worry will be not owning a car.

"Everyone's been worried about you," she says. "I know half of them just wanted the gory details, but seriously – we were all pretty scared."

I don't know what to say. What's the appropriate response for something like that? I just stay silent. After a while she makes a comment about Rachel and Adam being so boringly couple-ish, and we start talking about her love life. A reasonably safe topic, considering that it consists of her moaning about her single status and me reassuring her that someday she'll find someone perfect for her.

Art is where it happens.

We talk as we work. Everyone's doing something different. I'm painting, Rachel's sketching, others are doing lino printing. The idea is that we all have a couple of pieces finished by the end of the term, relating to a specific theme – we can choose from stuff like "Identity", "The Future" and "Love". It's pretty fun to do, way less stressful than the Junior Cert work. Art is the one class I actually like, and I'm starting to be glad I came into school today after all.

There's one particular asshole doing Art who goes by

the name of Simon Brady. (Si to his girlfriends, Brady to his mates, The Asshole to his exes. Don't ask. I was young and naïve.)

He struts over to me. I kid you not, *struts*. Then he just hovers there for a while, craning his neck like he's looking for something. I try to ignore him, but eventually snap, "What the hell do *you* want?"

"I was seeing if I could see the scars," he says innocently.

"What scars?" I ask oh-so-patiently, reminding myself that he's completely thick and I should feel sorry for him, really, and not be thinking about how great it would feel to smash his head against the wall.

"You know, the wrists? I heard you slashed them."

"You heard wrong."

"No, I don't think so. We all know you were rushed into hospital on Saturday."

"Get lost," I mutter.

"Why'd you do it, Nicole? Was it because you couldn't get some?"

It's not that I'm offended by the remark or that he's hit a nerve, it's just that he is *pissing me off*. I punch him in the stomach.

He's taken by surprise. "Hey! What the – you stupid bitch!"

He tries to hit me, but I duck.

"Simon! Jesus, what's going on here?" Miss Morgan demands, hurrying over to this side of the room.

"That *stupid bitch* –" he begins furiously.

"Watch your mouth," she reminds him.

"*Nicole*," he says, spitting out my name like it's a curse, "punched me."

I'm in deep shit now, I know.

"Right. And what did you do to deserve it?" she asks.

"Nothing!" he says innocently.

"Simon. I'm not stupid. She didn't punch you for no reason."

"How would you know? She's a psycho! She even tried to kill herself."

She doesn't look surprised. The whole staff probably knows. Mr Traynor even called my mum on Sunday, just to see how I was doing. I have yet to recover from the creepiness of him actually phoning my house to enquire about my well-being.

"Are you going to give me an answer or will I send you down to the principal?" she asks him.

Simon stares at her sullenly.

"You know where the office is," she shrugs.

He walks out, still doing his stupid arrogant strut, and slams the door behind him. And these are the sort of creatures I go to school with.

"Back to work, guys!" Miss Morgan tells the rest of the class, who have paused in the creation of their artistic endeavours to watch the drama unfold. Reluctantly, they resume being creative and productive, some more than others.

"Nicole, you'd better go down there as well," she sighs. "I know Simon's not exactly the most tactful person on earth, but you really shouldn't have punched him."

"It's fine," I shrug. "Getting into trouble is a small price to pay for being able to hit him."

She laughs. "How are you doing?" she asks seriously.

"Coping, so far," I nod.

"Good to hear it."

I smile, and head down to the office to face my doom.

33

Rachel

I hope she's not going to be in too much trouble. Simon was asking for it.

I get back to work on my "Identity" sketch, something I started today. It's a spiral of food with a girl sitting cross-legged in the middle of it all, looking miserable. It's completely crap. Nicole's the artistic one, and even Danielle, the girl who can only draw stick people, has more talent in her little finger than I do in my entire body.

Not for the first time, I start counting down the days until Art is over.

"Good work, Rachel," Miss Morgan comments, looking over my shoulder. "Is that supposed to be you?"

I shrug. "I don't know. Maybe."

She scrutinises the picture. "Why's she so depressed? Dieting for Christmas already?"

"Yeah, sort of. She wants to eat but she knows she'll feel guilty once she does."

(Shut up, Rachel, you don't need to keep babbling on . . .)

"She'll have to eat something, though. Otherwise she'll starve," she says lightly, and moves on to the guy next to me.

Nicole gets back to Art just before the bell goes for break.

"How'd it go?" I ask.

"Simon's got detention, and I was warned not to react so violently to stuff in future," she says.

"Was that it?"

"Yep. I think he was afraid that if he punished me for hitting Simon, I'd do something stupid. So, to avoid the guilt, he let me go free. Yay!"

I smile.

She looks at my now-completed picture. "Cool. It's sort of – I don't know. It makes you think."

"Thanks," I say in surprise. Well, I guess the thought behind it is a good one, even if my artistic ability leaves a lot to be desired.

At lunch, sitting outside, I'm beside Adam. Everyone seems to think of us as a couple already even though we're not really. We just flirt an awful lot. It's fun. I feel like I *matter*.

"You going to have anything to eat, Rache?" Nicole asks casually.

"Nah, not hungry," I lie. I am, of course, but if I eat something I'll have to throw up, and I promised myself I wasn't going to do that any more.

I am *dying* for something to eat, though. Maybe if I just

have something small – no. I can't do that, because something small leads onto something big and before I know it I'll have eaten tons. I can't risk it. I don't trust myself.

"Still, if you don't eat anything you might, you know, faint or something," she says.

"Nicole! Relax! I'm fine," I laugh, but I'm annoyed at her for pushing it, especially in front of everyone.

"You are sort of skinny, though," Adam says. "You should eat *something*."

I can't believe *he's* starting. Is the entire world against me?

"Thanks for that, Adam," I say, getting up. "If I wanted a lecture I would have gone to my *mother*."

"Hey, I was just *saying*," he protests, following me as I walk inside.

"Yeah. Whatever," I snap.

"Look, I don't know why you're so defensive."

"Defensive? I just don't like people nagging at me to eat!"

My stomach chooses this moment to growl.

"Hungry, huh?" he says. "Look, Rache, I don't know what's going on here, but this isn't normal. It's not like you *need* to be on a diet or anything."

"I know," I say. I do know. Didn't I decide that? So why am I still not eating?

Because it's bad, that's why.

"So why won't you eat something?" he pleads.

"I can't."

"Why not?"

"Because then I'll get fat."

"Eating lunch isn't going to make you fat. Eating too much is what does that, and there's no chance of that happening right now."

Eating *anything* is eating too much.

"My mom," he says, shifting awkwardly, "my mom – uh – she does counselling and stuff for like, eating disorders."

"So?" I say.

"Well, I'm not saying that you *have* one or anything, but you might want to talk to her or something. She'll be able to tell you how much you need to eat every day and stuff like that."

I shrug. I'm doing okay on my own. Right?

My stomach growls again.

"Just think about it," he suggests.

I'm ashamed to admit that in this important decision, his cuteness is the deciding factor.

"Okay," I nod, and grab onto the lifeline that's been thrown to me.

34

Danielle

Meet u on the green at 2. B there. Mark.

When I first get his text message, getting up, dressed and going out isn't part of my plan. But by the time two o'clock rolls around I'm out there.

I just didn't want him to be out there waiting for me all alone. Besides, it's easier to face Mark than it is everyone else. Even though I'm scared he's going to blame me for Nicole's – it's not your fault, it's not your fault. Even though there is that fear, I'm still dying to see him. He's taken up residence in my brain again, his voice commenting on things from time to time.

I see him and he's less . . . Mark than the Mark in my head. He's more human, less godlike. He has a spot on his chin. His hair is annoying me.

Still, I go over to him in spite of all his flaws. After all, no one's perfect. We hug, awkwardly.

"Why aren't you in school?" he asks.

"I'm just not," I say. Well, what is he expecting, the truth? I'm not in school because I've spent the last two days unable to get out of bed feeling like I wanted to drop off the face of the planet because I'm a horrible, horrible person and everything that can go wrong has gone wrong? And now that I'm out in the real world it feels weird and disorienting, and I want him to hurry up and say whatever he has to say so that I can retreat to my bed again? Yeah, I'm sure he'd love to hear *that*.

He might, actually, but only if he got to come back to bed with me.

"Why aren't you?" I counter.

"Didn't feel like it," he says.

"So, why did you drag me out here?" I ask.

Okay, "out here" is a bit dramatic for where we are, making it sound like Mars instead of down the road, but walking down here *felt* about as long as a journey to another planet.

"I wanted to talk to you about Nicole."

"Oh."

Which part? The Nicole-and-Mark part or the other Nicole thing? The horrible one, the awful one. Please, don't talk about that one, Mark.

"Someone kinda told me you were upset about me and Nicole meeting on Junior Cert night," he says.

"Really, who?" I ask coolly. "They were probably lying."

"Rachel."

"Oh." *Rachel!* She never told me. I'm going to kill her.

"I was talking to her on Saturday, right before Caitlin came over."

Relief. He has a perfectly legitimate excuse for being at my house with Rachel on Saturday – discussing me. The arm is another story, but I'll give him the benefit of the doubt on that one.

"Yeah. Well, I'm fine. I was just really emotional that night. All the drink." I'm trying to sound nonchalant but I'm pretty sure I'm failing miserably.

"Oh, right. I just wanted to make sure you were okay with it."

"Why wouldn't I be?" I ask innocently.

He shrugs. "I don't know. I thought it might be weird for me to meet one of your best friends."

She's not one of my best friends any more. Friends don't drive friends to . . . it's not your fault!

"It's fine, it doesn't really matter."

"Good," he says. "It's not like I'm with her or anything, anyway. I sort of like someone else."

"Who is it?" I ask, trying to stay calm.

"I'm not telling," he grins.

"Please?"

"Nope."

"Pretty please?"

"Nope."

"Pretty please and I'll sleep with you if you tell me?"

"Temptress," he laughs. "But I'm still not telling."

"Is it someone I know, at least?"

"Yeah, you know her," he says.

See? Doesn't that sound like he could be talking about me? I bet he really is. I *hope* he really is.

"Do you think Nicole wants to go out with me, though?" he asks.

"You're full of yourself," I grin.

"Nah, I'm just wondering if she was looking for more than a meet. The last thing I want to do is to upset her, especially after what happened."

"Yeah," I say lifelessly.

Why did you have to bring it up, Mark?

Maybe it was a pointed comment. Not wanting to upset her. Is that what we all should have been doing before it happened? If we'd been more understanding, maybe she wouldn't have done it.

I hate her for making me feel guilty. I didn't do anything! I shouldn't *have* to feel guilty. But I do.

I hate you, Nicole, for making me feel this way. I really do.

35

Nicole

I hate being a victim.

I *hate* getting special treatment from the principal. I punched a guy. I want to be punished. I don't want people pretending to understand me when they don't. I don't want to get off with a warning, I want to be treated like I would have been normally. Get yelled at, get a detention, maybe even get suspended.

I hate people being afraid to upset me. I hate the way they're scared to make any references to death or anything that might "offend" me. Someone said, "I'm dying to go home" and then looked at me in absolute horror. "God, Nicole, I'm so sorry!" I hadn't even picked up on it. It didn't bother me. I'm not some delicate flower who'll break if you mention something upsetting. I never have been.

Sure, I have my soft side, but very few people get to see that. In school they know me as tough, and I'm missing that. Suddenly I'm being thought of as a crazy over-sensitive freak. If they keep it up I really *will* go crazy.

Rachel doesn't speak to me after lunch. I think she's still annoyed with me for bringing up the topic of her not eating. I suppose it wasn't the best place for it, but I'm worried about her. There was this girl I saw in the hospital who was going through chemotherapy for some form of cancer, and she'd lost loads of weight as a result. Rachel reminds me of her. She's just as thin. It can't be good.

When I go home I'm bored, and restless, and just generally feeling fed up of my life. I end up drinking. That always seems to work. There's no one here to stop me. Luke's out with his friends, Val's probably shopping, the parents are at work.

My life's terrible, I decide. Awful, really. Who'd want to be me? No one. And no one should be forced to endure it.

I feel very sorry for myself.

Mum has thrown out her sleeping pills.

She finally did something intelligent, I think. Of course this makes it harder for me. How thoughtless of her.

She hates me, you know. She really hates me. She likes Val better. She wishes Val was her real daughter.

Nobody loves me. Nobody in the entire world.

Slice. Slice.

36

Rachel

Danielle's in bed when I get home. No surprise there. I don't know why she stays there, or whether it's her twisted way of getting attention or not, but right now I'm not too concerned. I'm thinking about Adam's mother. He said he'd talk to her and that I could probably have a chat with her tomorrow after school.

It's sweet that he's so concerned. Even if I don't want him knowing how bad it really is.

I spend about half an hour daydreaming about Adam before snapping back to reality. I'm utterly starving. How about an apple? That's okay, right? No, wait, it's got natural sugar, which means calories, which means fat. Nothing's safe.

I go up to Danielle's room, not out of any great concern for her, but to distract myself.

"Hey!" I greet her.

"What do you want?" she asks.

"World peace. Why won't you get out of bed?"

"Leave me alone."

"Make me. Why?"

"Rachel, *go!*"

"Just tell me!" I say. "You must have a *reason*."

I know that I'm playing the clichéd pesky younger sister, and I cringe. It's almost enough to make me want to throw up, if I had anything left in my stomach.

"I don't want to get up, that's why," she says.

"Life's not that bad, Danielle."

"Yes, it *is*."

"Nicole manages to get out of bed in the mornings."

Danielle's face contorts at the mention of Nicole, almost in pain.

"You should call round to see her, you know," I tell her.

"I don't want to."

"I don't think she's mad at you any more. And I don't think she blames you, either."

"Why would she blame me? I haven't done anything wrong!" Danielle insists.

Okay, there goes *my* theory. So much for thinking she was sick with guilt.

"I mean, *she* meets the guy I like, *she* says horrible things to all of us, and I'm the one who's meant to feel guilty?" she demands.

"No one said you're meant to feel guilty," I say, puzzled.

"Yeah, well, I do," she snaps.

And now I start to get it. She *is* feeling guilty, but she thinks she shouldn't, so she's annoyed with Nicole, but also upset . . . no, forget it. My sister's psyche is way too complex for me to understand, but I half-know what she's talking about.

"Nicole was the one who took the pills," I say gently.

"I know! And I can't believe she – I mean, how could she be so *stupid*? She's got the perfect life, and she does this for – what? *Attention?*"

"Maybe. Maybe not."

"And it's like she didn't even *think* about what she'd be putting all of *us* through. I mean, did she really think that just because we'd had a fight we'd be *glad* if she died?"

Danielle starts to cry, and I hold her, my own worries (almost) completely forgotten. She's just as upset as the rest of us were, maybe even more, but I never thought she was. I took for granted that she wasn't affected by it at all. I mean, logically I *knew* that she wasn't hiding in bed for no reason, but I didn't *think*.

"She's okay, you know," I whisper. "That's the important thing. She's okay and now we can all be friends again."

"Yay." She smiles weakly.

"Did you know Adam's mum counsels people with eating disorders?" I ask.

She shakes her head. "No. Are you going to go talk to her?"

"Yeah. Do you think I should?"

"I think you're exactly the sort of person she counsels, if that's what you mean," she says quietly.

"You're overreacting," I tell her.

164

"Am I?" she asks, staring at me.

The phone rings. I go and answer the one in my parents' bedroom.

"Hello?"

"Rachel? Rache, is that you?"

"Yeah, it's me. Nicole?"

"There's blood everywhere." She's crying. "Rache, I'm scared." She also sounds drunk.

"What did you do?" I demand, feeling my heart pound faster and my world spin into nightmare-land. Again.

"Simon's going to be pretty happy about this," she giggles.

Oh God, she's done her wrists. How long does it take for that to – I mean, how long does she have? I keep thinking of that scene with Glenn Close in *Fatal Attraction*.

"Nicole, I'm going to call an ambulance, okay?" I say.

"Okay," she hiccups.

I hang up the phone and then dial. Danielle comes into the room. "Who was it?" she asks.

"Nicole," I answer, and then give the information over the phone. "She called me just a second ago. She's slit her wrists."

Danielle gasps. As I give the address I watch her lean against the wall in shock. I know how she feels. Once I'm finished, we race over to Nicole's, hoping and praying frantically that she'll survive.

Part Four

Recovery

37

Danielle

My first words to Nicole are "You stupid bitch!"

I admit it's a pretty dramatic scene, me striding into her room at the hospital and shouting at the poor girl lying in the bed with her wrists bandaged up.

"What were you *thinking*? Didn't you learn anything from the first time? God, Nicole, why did you go and do something as *ridiculous* as this?"

"Nice to see you too, Danielle," she half-smiles.

Her lack of an emotional response calms me down a little bit, and frankly, I'm so relieved that she's okay that I can't be angry any more.

I sit down. "Why'd you do it, Nic?" I ask. Oh, God, I'm going to cry. This is awful. I feel like I'm in a soap.

"My therapist thinks it was a cry for help," she says.

"Your *therapist?*" I smirk.

She giggles. "Yep. I feel so American. Do you actually

know anyone who sees a therapist? I mean, God! She's not as bad as I thought she'd be, though."

"So, is she right? About the cry-for-help thing."

Nicole shrugs. "No idea. Mostly she just asks me about school and my family and stuff, but you can tell that she's always thinking about why I did it, and she just doesn't want to say so. I tried telling her that I was drunk and didn't know what I was doing, but she won't accept it. She's like, 'But *why* were you drinking? Do you often turn to alcohol as a solution to your problems?' It wrecks my head."

"But at least you'll be able to figure out why you did it, right?" I ask.

She nods. "That's the basic idea."

"You must *know*, though."

"Yeah. I know I wanted it to be over." She looks at me. "You ever felt that way?"

"Yep."

"How's Mark?"

"Less cute than he was."

"Ah. Bye-bye, rose-tinted glasses; hello, harsh reality, huh?"

"Something like that. I don't know, it was weird – I saw him today, and we talked, and he seemed so *normal*. Just like everyone else we hang around with."

"What, did you think he was really an alien or something?" she smiles.

"No, I just thought he was perfect."

"No one's perfect," she says matter-of-factly.

Yeah. I know that. I just *think* that they are. And then

when they fall from the pedestal I've placed them on, I can't handle it. That's what I did with Rachel, with Nicole, with Mark. He's not perfect. When they say that absence makes the heart grow fonder they're right, but only because when you're not with someone all the time you forget about their faults and concentrate solely on their good points. Then you magnify and exaggerate them, so that you create this hero in your mind.

I know I should've gotten over Mark a long time ago. I'm not sure why I didn't. Maybe it was just easier for me to dwell on what might have been instead of moving on. I could have the safety of fancying someone without it being spoiled by actually going out with them. Who knows, maybe he *is* the Romeo to my Juliet and in ten years' time we'll end up married. But right now I'm going to try to move on. And in fairness, I have tried already. It was just that every time I thought I might be getting over him, I told myself that it was only temporary and that sooner or later I'd be crazy about him again. So I was.

I'm annoyed with myself, really, for wasting so much time on him. Especially after the text message that came earlier – I wasn't able to appreciate the humour of it until I knew Nicole was okay.

I hand over my phone to Nicole. "Read the first message in the inbox," I instruct.

She reads aloud. "'Okay, I'll tell you. I was talking about Naomi.' Was this today?"

"Uh-huh. He was telling me that he doesn't want to go out with you –"

"Oh, thank God," Nicole says.

" – because he fancies someone else."

"Don't tell me he's interested in Naomi!" Nicole says.

We start laughing.

"*This* is the guy we fought over!" I say through giggles.

"I can't believe it!"

When we finally stop, I look at her. "Sorry for being a bitch."

"Me too."

"Let's never fight again," I kid.

"Oh, yeah, we'll keep to *that*," she says, rolling her eyes.

"Okay, let's never fight over a guy again," I suggest.

"It depends on the guy," she grins.

"Never fight over Mark again?"

"Deal!" she agrees enthusiastically.

"I didn't meet him to hurt you or force you to get over him or anything," she tells me later.

"Why did you?"

"Stupid reasons. I saw him as my knight in shining armour or something. I went outside with this guy Niall, right? I knew him from the summer, and anyway . . . he had more on his mind than just meeting."

"God. Do you think that's why –"

"I don't know," she shrugs. "It didn't help. Anyway, so I go back inside and who do I see? Mark. So I'm so grateful to have a strong guy there to protect me that I fool myself into thinking that I'm madly in love with him – remember that I'm totally pissed at this point – and I just *go* for him."

So that's what really happened. Poor Nicole. I never realised that she had all this stuff going on. I just thought – well, that she had the perfect life.

I'm incredibly deluded, I know. From now on I'm going to accept the fact that everyone has hidden depths. It's kind of scary, though, when you realise that you don't know people as well as you thought you did.

I remember thinking on the first day of school that we all looked so innocent in our uniforms and it was funny because we weren't sheltered from the world. I look back and cringe at my arrogance now. We were – at least, *I* was. I thought that eating disorders were things that happened to other people and not your own sister. I thought that people who tried to kill themselves had no friends and were ugly and had obviously awful lives. I thought that the biggest worry I had was whether Mark liked me or not. And now things have changed so much.

Just as I'm thinking these terribly deep, profound thoughts, a cute male nurse comes into the room and I check him out. Yum.

Maybe things haven't changed that much after all . . .

38

Nicole

I don't remember much. What I do remember is vague and disturbing. Blood all over the kitchen floor and staining the silver of a stainless steel knife. People trying to stop the bleeding – Rachel and Danielle, who came in through the back door. Being in the ambulance and feeling unworthy of their time and energy. And then waking up and feeling like shit.

As bad as I felt, I knew that this was it. This was life. I wasn't Little Miss Sunshine and infused with false happiness like I had been the last time. Everything wasn't miraculously okay now.

It's going to take work. Talking to my eternally-looking-for-a-deeper-meaning therapist, for a start. ("And how did that make you *feel*, Nicole?") And I'm giving up drinking, definitely. That's part of the problem, I know that much. I get depressed, I drink; I get even more depressed, I wind up in hospital. I don't want the rest of my life to be like that. I intend on getting out of here as soon as possible.

I guess what I've learned is that there's no quick fix. You can't make your problems go away with drinking or drugs or even a big sharp knife. Because either you end up in here, your problems as real as they ever were, or you end up dead. And who wants that? They want the pain to go away, but they don't want to die. At least that's what I think. That's what I wanted.

It's a relief to know that I don't have to worry about hurting Mark. He wasn't interested in anything deeper any more than I was. It *is* pretty funny that he's into Naomi, though. Of all the people . . .

Speaking of Naomi, she visited earlier on. She forgives me for being so blunt, which is good, but has let me know in no uncertain terms that if I ever so much as try to treat her like that again, she will make sure I'm in hospital for a very, very long time.

How sweet.

Michelle and Eric were in to see me, too. Michelle hasn't mentioned Junior Cert night so I'd like to *assume* she's forgiven me. Aaagh. It's all so complicated. Plus, I'm still sort of jealous of her. Oh, well, no one said life was perfect, right?

39

Rachel

As planned, I talk to Adam's mum on Tuesday after school. It's not formal, just a chat, but I'm still nervous. By Tuesday afternoon my nails are bitten down into nothingness.

She turns out to be really friendly and easy to talk to. What a relief. I leave feeling in control. Not in control in the scary controlling-calorie-intake-obsessively kind of way, but in a good way. Like, it's my life, and I can take control.

I am empowered.

Adam rolls his eyes when I see him afterwards. "Oh, God. She's created a monster."

"I am *empowered*," I announce, and then crack up laughing at his horrified expression. "Oh, come on, I'm not *that* bad."

We're still not *together*, but according to everyone we behave like we are. I don't mind, really. For the moment we're flirty friends, and there's no pressure, but plenty of fun. So it's good. I don't think I'm ready to jump into a relationship right now – I think I need to sort out my own life before entangling it with someone else's.

I know it's going to take a while to get things back to normal, if they ever can go back. That's a pretty scary thought, actually, never going back to normal. Maybe it's that, more than anything (apart from Adam's looks, of course) that made me realise I had to get help from *somewhere*. Maybe it was the thing with Nicole that shocked me into it. Maybe all this analysis of my life is giving me a headache.

Okay, enough maybes. Here are the facts: I think Adam is cute. I love the people in my life. I'm lucky to be alive. You need food to live. Grades aren't everything.

And the most important truth of all: right now, I'm happy.

God, that sounds cheesy . . . how about this for an important truth? Chocolate is delicious. I had two squares today, broken off from a bar Danielle was munching on. I would have had more, but . . . well, I was saving room for my dinner.

THE END

Dear Diary
by
Claire Hennessy

5 friends
5 diaries,
5 months
They've got it all down.
But do they really know each other?

Boyfriends, slumber-parties and stepsisters:
In 5 months
& 5 diaries,
5 friends

Come a long way.

Get the inside story from brilliant
young author Claire Hennessy.

ISBN: 1-85371-917-X
Poolbeg - The *Irish* For Bestsellers!

· Being Her Sister
by
Claire Hennessy

*What do you do when life is all about
being her sister?*

*When, no matter what you do, you end
up being compared to her?*

*"I mean, if you had a younger sister like
Rachel who was better than you at
everything, wouldn't you be depressed?"*

*"Danielle's so popular. Yeah, even my friends
think she's the greatest. But they don't have
to shove it in my face."*

ISBN: 1-84223-017-4

Poolbeg - The *Irish* For Bestsellers!